AF485585

The Colonel
and
Miss Bennet

A Pride and
Prejudice Variation

Joseph P. Garland

DermodyHouse.com

The Cover:

The Officer is *Major John Biddle*, painted in 1818 by Thomas Scully.
It is at the Metropolitan Museum.
metmuseum.org/art/collection/search/12692

The lady is also at the Met. She is *Mrs. Robert Dickey* (Anne Brown), painted by John Wesley Jarvis between 1807 and 1810.
https://www.metmuseum.org/art/collection/search/1 1249

Introduction

This is a *Pride and Prejudice* Sequel. I have attempted to retain everything contained in Miss Austen's novel other than moving the story later than in the book (although there is a debate as to when the story in the book takes place).

Although I call it a *sequel*, the first part of the book covers territory in the original, that being from when Darcy and Col. Fitzwilliam went to Rosings Park through the Darcy and Bingley weddings.

Where I have erred with regard to the original, please feel free to inform me of this villainous act. Each is the result of my error, for which I peremptorily apologize.

The quotation at page 83 in Chapter 14 is from the June 26, 1815 edition of the *Observer*, which was quoted in a June 18, 2015 (i.e., two hundred years after the battle) article by Richard Nellson in *The Guardian* entitled How the Observer Reported the Battle of Waterloo.

There is additional historic information about that battle referenced at the end, at page 212

Joseph P. Garland

1.

"Am I right to suppose that Miss Elizabeth Bennet is the reason for our sudden visit to the insufferable parson so soon after our arrival?"

"I do not understand your meaning."

"You are so inept at shielding your feelings, at least to an old cousin like me, Darcy. The parson is a dullard, and his wife is overly dutiful to him. Her father and sister are ciphers. That leaves only the fifth. Do you deny that Miss Bennet was the attraction?"

There were few people in the world who could speak to Fitzwilliam Darcy in such a manner. One of them was walking beside him as they crossed the slightly rising lawn to the great house at Rosings Park. That was Colonel Richard Fitzwilliam. He and Darcy were cousins—the colonel's titled father was Darcy's late mother's brother—and they were nearly the same age.

Both were tall, though the colonel was not handsome and Darcy was and the colonel was comfortable with the social graces and Darcy was not.

They had arrived at Rosings Park, the estate of their aunt, Lady Catherine de Bourgh, the day before. Indeed, as their carriage passed the Hunsford Parsonage en route, the clergyman had given the moving carriage a deep bow before rushing inside to provide his wife and their visitors (that is, Mrs. Collins's father and younger sister Maria and the aforementioned Miss Bennet) with the news that Lady Catherine's nephew Darcy had arrived, as had long been expected.

Elizabeth had met that gentleman before, when she was home at Longbourn in Hertfordshire. There, she had come to the widely shared opinion that he was a most proud and disagreeable man. Now, in Kent, she happened herself to be visiting her great friend Charlotte, née Lucas, who had married Elizabeth's own cousin, William Collins. The couple resided at the Parsonage.

Though Elizabeth had not been with the Collinses for long, the appearance of someone new, even someone as disagreeable as Fitzwilliam Darcy, could not help but enliven the staleness that had quickly descended on her.

And it was on the morning after the two men's arrival that the two cousins had their discussion about Miss Bennet. On that morning, Mr. Collins had hastened very early and very excitedly to the great house to pay his respects. When he got there, he had discovered that Darcy had been joined on his visit by a second of Lady Catherine's nephews, this Colonel Fitzwilliam. Mr. Collins carried the bone to Lady Catherine's that Miss Elizabeth Bennet was visiting. With that tidbit, Darcy spontaneously and, it must be said, quite out of character insisted that the colonel join him in returning to the Parsonage with Mr. Collins. And that is how Colonel Fitzwilliam came to meet Elizabeth Bennet and how the officer came to suspect his cousin's particular...interest in that fine woman after they sat for tea and cakes offered by their hosts.

And the officer displayed the quality of his breeding by easily falling into conversation with Elizabeth and the Collinses and even with Charlotte's father and sister.

Ellizabeth saw at once the contrast between the cousins. For other than inquiring about the state of Miss Bennet's family, Darcy sat mute until being slightly unsettled when she asked whether he had met her sister Jane in town. For some months, Jane had been staying in London, at their aunt and uncle's house in Cheapside.

He averred that he had not had the pleasure of seeing Jane Bennet in town, and it was not long after that that the two gentlemen left and took their walk back to the house. During which the colonel challenged Darcy about the attractions of Miss Elizabeth Bennet.

As they neared the house, Darcy relented.

"I cannot say what it is, Richard. But it is something. She is so...so...inappropriate and perhaps I take some strange, bizarre enjoyment from simply being with her."

"At least I will say that she does seem to have an effect on you. But why were you so...unsociable with her?"

"It is my way. You know that full well."

"Indeed, I do. Perhaps you will do better when you are again with her. She strikes me as the type of woman who will improve with familiarity."

"I have found her to be so."

With that the two had reached the house and after an inquiry and being told that neither Lady Catherine nor her daughter Anne was downstairs, they went to their rooms to prepare to go for a late morning ride about the grounds.

*   *   *   *

The charms of Miss Elizabeth Bennet could not help but extend to Colonel Richard Fitzwilliam. He found the lady's presence could work wonders to what he feared would become a tedious stretch at Rosings Park. As a result, after that first, spontaneous visit, he began to stop by the Parsonage regularly without Darcy. He did not conceal the fact and was surprised that his friend expressed no interest in joining him. And on each of his visits, the officer enjoyed sitting with his tea and cakes and conversed easily with Miss Elizabeth and Mrs. Collins and even, when he was there, with Mr. Collins himself.

He found neither Sir William nor Maria Lucas was capable of participating in any but the most staccato fashion. They were perfectly content to eat, drink, and observe with quite a measure, thought the colonel, of idiocy.

He found, too, that Elizabeth Bennet was worlds apart from all the others, as he discovered a fair amount about her, expressed in a natural and always matter-of-fact style, quite at odds with the normal course of conversation of women in the colonel's experience.

Early on, when they were seated at the Parsonage near one another, unlikely to be overheard, she spoke of the difficulties of her family's situation, what with her father's estate being entailed to the closest male relation, he and his wife having only girls and five of them (of which Elizabeth was the second), and of Mr. Collins himself being that closest male relation thus destined to inherit the family's estate in Hertfordshire.

"So you see, Colonel, I am hardly a catch and with my aunt's husband a country lawyer and my uncle a tradesman in Cheapside my shortcomings will be hard for a man to overlook."

"A lesser man, perhaps." He smiled and leaned in the slightest bit closer to her. "In any case, I can assure you, Miss Bennet, that being a son is not as lucrative as one might hope. You see, I am a second son. My brother will inherit the estate and my father's title and I was fortunate to have been given the means of acquiring a commission."

"So you have done well, Colonel," interjected Charlotte.

"Ah, Mrs. Collins," he said, as he directed his attention to her, "it is not all parading, I'm afraid. We look quite resplendent in our regimentals, I grant you, with our men marching or riding in step beside us. But we are a nation that has long been at war. We may be done with Bonaparte, but the war in America continues."

"And have you been in the wars? What about the militia?" asked Maria, displaying a sudden interest in the talk. "They came to Meryton."

He turned to the naïve girl. "Well, the militia is meant to provide some protection while we real soldiers are off doing our soldiering. While I may have been easily enough able to myself avoid serving as, well, a *real* soldier and remained a martinet as others have, I decided to do my duty. So, yes, I was on the Peninsula for quite a while and saw more action as a soldier than I ever wish to, thank you."

"But," Elizabeth asked as her eyes inspected his body, "were you injured? It must have been horrible."

His attention shifted back. "Miss Bennet, ladies, Sir William, it is something for us and you should set your minds at ease. We are in the service of King and Country, and we do so willingly. I have been fortunate. And I hope to remain so."

He took a final sip of his tea. The others remained silent until their guest stood, and they followed. He bid them all a *good day* with a tight bow. And soon they watched him cross to the gate that opened to the path that led back to the great house, and Elizabeth gave a thought to what it would be like to be married to a soldier.

For his part, as he reached the lawn, the colonel recognised not for the first time that the visit to his aunt was greatly enhanced by the fortuitous presence at Rosings of Miss Bennet.

In the following days, Elizabeth continued to cherish the solitude of her exploration of the many varied paths in Rosings Park. She was slightly rattled on one of the first of these turns, though, when she happened upon Mr. Darcy himself. It came as quite a surprise, then, when she found being alone with him for the first time was not entirely unpleasant. Or at least not nearly as unpleasant as she would have imagined it would be had she ever thought it might take place, which she assuredly had not. Nothing of consequence was said by either. Elizabeth thought little of it except that only a few days later, she was on a different path when they came upon one another again. And again they walked, albeit a little longer, and again little of substance was said.

Any doubt that these rendezvouses were not a coincidental consequence of their both apparently being fond of walking in the Kentish air was erased when it happened for a third time in yet another part of the Park. Elizabeth did not know why but for some reason this unsettled her. It seemed that her pleasure in walking alone on the beautiful, verdant paths was somehow affected by these encounters. She mentioned it to Charlotte when she was back at the Parsonage. Her friend left no doubt as to Mr. Darcy's obvious attentions to Miss Bennet. Though Elizabeth firmly disagreed *to her friend*, insisting that there was not the slightest thing suspicious about it all, to herself, she was not so certain. She would not, either way, allow whatever was motivating Mr. Darcy to alter what had become a most pleasant diversion to her for this extended visit to the Collinses'.

Her resolve was soon tested. On yet another path, Then, on the next day but one, during her walk she espied a lone figure, a gentleman, nearing her. She quickly recognized the jaunty step as not being Darcy's and surmised, correctly, that it was his cousin's.

As the colonel approached, he lifted his hat and waved his switch and appeared genuinely pleased about seeing her on what, he would tell her, was an annual survey of his aunt's estate. She, too, was happy and redirected her own steps towards him, matching his smile.

"I am most pleased to see you," he said, receiving the truthful "And I you" in response.

The two fell into a relaxed conversation, one quite different from the strained exchanges that she and Darcy tended to have, especially during their recent walks.

Elizabeth and the colonel found their words drifting inevitably to Darcy. The colonel admitted his envy of his cousin in his ability, thanks to his *money*, to do what he wished to do when he wished to do it and with whom.

"But you will admit that you have put yourself in a position in which you have made yourself dependent upon him to live the pleasant life you find yourself living," she pointed out.

"Save for my time in the wars. Yes, it is my fate and perhaps even my choice that has placed me where I find myself. But to be honest, Miss Bennet, for me to be taken off Darcy's hands, I should need a woman with at least forty thousand if I am to marry her. Perhaps even fifty."

She smiled. "Indeed, though I have not acquired such expensive tastes as you appear to have, I too cannot afford to marry anything that is not at least a small fortune."

He placed his arm through hers. "Then, I fear, we are never fated to be husband and wife."

"I fear that you are correct."

"So, nature and fate force each of us in the end to fend for ourselves."

"If," she responded, "we cannot rely on the kindness of Fitzwilliam Darcy or a similarly generous patron."

"Indeed, Miss Bennet. Indeed. And I assure you that he is among the finest gentlemen of my acquaintance."

She found his statement, albeit one made with far longer knowledge and kinship, quite at odds with her own view of the man. "That is not my experience with him, but that has been quite brief and far from intimate.

I would like to know what you can mean." She would allow herself to hear what evidence the officer would present to establish his claim.

And he endeavored to provide it. He spoke of seeing his cousin often when they were both young, with him at Pemberley in Derbyshire and he not so far away at his father's estate of Haverford Hall in Lincolnshire. "I will concede," he told her, "that Pemberley is the superior of my family's run-down place, built in the reign of who-cares-who and altered rather poorly in the centuries since."

They might have taken a more direct route to the Parsonage, but they veered off several times to extend their enjoyment of each other's company.

"You may not know that his mother, who was my father's and Lady Catherine's sister, died many years ago leaving his father to raise both Darcy and Georgiana, a girl much younger than he and I. It was quite difficult for her, being without a mother. Then when their father died some five years ago, he and I became her guardian, though Darcy much more than me."

She had heard this sister mentioned at Netherfield, especially by Caroline Bingley, as being quite an accomplished girl. "What can you tell me of this Georgiana?"

"She is a tall girl, a woman really, though, she is not yet eighteen, and is very shy owing, I think, to the circumstance of losing her mother when she was very young and spending much time in the country and I think being doted on."

"Does she not go to town?"

"There was a time, Miss Bennet, when we arranged for her to be established in London with a governess but...but that did not prove agreeable and thus she resumed her residency at Pemberley with several governesses and tutors to educate her."

Elizabeth had a sudden interest in this stranger.

"And how was she educated?"

"I expect it was the way all such well-off daughters are educated. But in one respect, though I believe for different reasons, she appears quite like her brother, in having great difficulty with the social graces."

"He admitted as much about himself when we were recently at Lady Catherine's fine pianoforte."

"He did indeed, Miss Bennet, and if memory serves, you chided him for it and I believe your words pained and perhaps even cut him, though I do not think it was too deep for a stubborn old soul like Fitzwilliam Darcy and"—he put up his hand to quiet Elizabeth—"it was surely not unwarranted."

"Though perhaps in some small degree." She well recalled it, when he claimed his awkwardness was a defense and she did no more than observe that it was more his own failure to attempt to overcome it. She was surprised that the colonel said her remark had some impact on his pompous cousin.

As the walk eventually found the tired pair nearing the Parsonage, the colonel played his final card in support of his cousin and gave her proof of how faithful he was as a friend, in saving Charles Bingley from a most inappropriate match with a woman of questionable relations, to which proof she listened silently.

"So, you see, Miss Bennet, that Darcy is not entirely the stiff, unfeeling figure I believe you to have taken him for."

They were approaching the opening in Rosings Park that took them to the Hunsford Road and the Parsonage.

As they reached the house, she removed her arm from her guide and turned to him.

"Colonel Fitzwilliam, I am most obliged by your observations. Mr. Darcy surely is well served by his friends."

With that, they exchanged courtesies, and she was inside and he was back through the gate and pleased with himself for the course of their conversation as he headed to Lady Catherine's great house. He even began to regret that he and Darcy had planned to leave Rosings Park in three days' time and would thereby lose the company of this fine, if unattainable (for him), woman.

It was even more painful, then, when the very next evening, Lady Catherine's two guests sat after dinner in a pair of comfortable chairs in the house's fine library after dinner, Darcy said he at least was leaving a day early.

"Good God, man. Why this sudden need to go?"

"I will not impose on you, Richard. You may stay if you wish. Lady Catherine and Anne will, I'm sure, be most pleased by your continued presence. As for me, though, there is some pressing business I must attend to."

"Pressing business? Have you received some sort of dispatch calling you to town? To Pemberley?"

"I do not wish to talk about it. It must suffice to you that I say I must leave, and I must leave without any further delay. I have waited too long as it is. But, again, you may remain."

"Do not be absurd. You know I rely on you and, worse, that I would be far worse off being left here alone. You are at least a buffer with our aunt. So, I will leave, but I wish you would confide in me as to why we go so soon."

Darcy reached over as they were preparing to go to their rooms.

"I cannot tell you, my friend. But you must believe me when I say it cannot be helped. It is a matter of a possible entanglement that I perhaps someday will be able to explain to you. Just not yet."

With that, he left the colonel alone and went to his aunt's room to inform her of the change in intentions.

After a somber dinner and evening, the colonel happened to see his friend leave the house early the next morning, heading in the general direction of the Parsonage and appearing to have some type of letter gripped in his right hand. His stride was purposeful, the colonel thought, and he wondered whether that letter had anything to do with the sudden decision to leave and he speculated that it likely did.

About an hour later, the colonel visited the Parsonage. When he arrived, Mrs. Collins said that Mr. Darcy had already been there and had told them that he and the colonel would be leaving the next morning. Asked about Miss Bennet, Charlotte said she had gone out early herself and since she was gone for quite a while, even more than usual, she must soon be coming back.

But after waiting for well over half an hour in a high degree of awkwardness, the colonel stood and gave his own goodbyes and expressed his own disappointment about not being able to do so personally to Miss Bennet herself.

"Alas," he said as he reached the gate with Mr. and Mrs. Collins. "Time waits for no man, especially for an old soldier such as myself, and I must be off. Perhaps I will stumble upon Miss Bennet on my way to the house but if I do not, please be sure to express my great disappointment about not having the opportunity to say goodbye to her myself."

Final goodbyes were exchanged as he left. In the event, he did not meet Miss Elizabeth Bennet as he returned across the lawn to the great house.

*   *   *   *

So, with neither gentleman having seen the object of both of their interests (at least at the Parsonage), they were gone the next morning, riding in the fine curricle in which they had arrived, which would convey them the twenty miles or so to Darcy's house on Brook Street in London. Their departure was witnessed by Mr. Collins much as their arrival had been and he hurried to the Parsonage to spread the news before rushing to the great house to console Lady Catherine and Miss Anne on their great loss.

It happened that the day before the two left for London, Elizabeth Bennet had indeed been wandering for some time on various of Rosings Park's paths reading that letter that Darcy had indeed written to her, and carried delicately and deliberately from the great house, and delivered to her when he came upon her on one of the estate's paths, delivered in a very formal and hurried manner by its author. She spent quite a while contemplating what the correspondence meant. It was written in a harsh, confident hand filling two pages and attempting to justify certain conduct that Elizabeth had cited to in the end impugn Darcy's character when he had proposed marriage to her suddenly and, to her, inexplicably. And when she had finished her third or fourth read as she sat on an old tree stump, with increased but ill-defined emotions each time and its specifics nearly burned into her, she could not help but chastise herself for *some* of the judgments she had made about Darcy.

But softened as her view of Fitzwilliam Darcy might have been in some respects, particularly as it concerned one George Wickham, whose integrity was more suspect than he made it appear when he was paying her attention from shortly after he had arrived at Meryton as part of the militia, it did not signify. Darcy had proposed to her in a most unappealing manner, protesting that he loved her and wished to marry her against all reason and regard for his and his family's will and reputation. To Miss Bennet, that deficiency in his character remained unaltered, even as her critical view of him in other respects was now suspect thanks to his letter. It hardly mattered. She had rejected him, and he would soon be gone from Rosings, and she thought it unlikely that she would see him or his cousin ever again.

Which would be for the best.

When she returned to the Parsonage after her walk with the letter safely stored in one of her pockets and was told of the gentlemen's changed plans and even more when the next day brought the news from Mr. Collins that the two gentlemen had left Lady Catherine's estate for London, she said "good riddance" to herself and expected that memories of the two would be quickly banished.

About a week later, on the morning after a final dinner at the great house, Elizabeth and the Lucases said their own goodbyes to Lady Catherine and to Mr. and Mrs. Collins and returned to Meryton and Longbourn. And when they reached their homes, matters resumed largely as they always had been, particularly when Jane returned from Cheapside barely a week later. Elizabeth thought it best to say nothing to her sister about what she had spoken of and learned from Darcy. It being for the best.

2.

Darcy had sent an express to London the day before. When he and the colonel reached his house in the late morning, the servants were ready for them. After the gentlemen made themselves presentable, they were famished and dug into a buffet that had been set up in the sitting room on a server with breads and meats and cheeses. The two were left alone to make their meals as they would, with a healthy pair of tankards with a fine Yorkshire ale. They moved a pair of table chairs near the window with a small, scalloped table between them so they could watch a bit of Mayfair pass while they ate and drank at their leisure.

Once settled, Darcy said, "I owe you a bit of an explanation."

"You owe me nothing, Darcy."

Darcy ignored this. As they rode to town, he had firmly resolved to be forthcoming, speak to his friend and admit the cause of their fleeing Kent.

"I have proposed to Miss Elizabeth Bennet."

The colonel stopped mid-chew and used a napkin to shield his surprise. He made no reply.

Darcy stood.

"It did not go well. Hence our sudden evacuation."

"What do you mean, *it did not go well?*" The colonel put his fork on the plate that he had balanced on his lap as he watched his cousin, who had begun pacing, as was his wont when his natural equilibrium was upset. He stopped and looked at the colonel.

"I will actually say that it went far worse than *not well.*" He resumed his seat. "Proposing to a woman is not something, you understand, with which I have any experience. It was made worse by my being somewhat...undiplomatic in my words."

"Your frankness generally does you credit, Darcy, but there are moments when a bit of tact would help rather than hinder your cause."

"Of course, I *know* that. But in such a moment, I truly felt I could not be false to a lady who I have come to deeply admire as a woman."

"You are confessing that you have discovered a deep love for Elizabeth Bennet?"

"And only with her, yes." He again was on his legs. "I fought it because all spoke against it as did her circumstances. Only Bingley would have had an encouraging word had I spoken to him about it, which I did not."

"Her lack of a fortune? It happens that she and I spoke of *that*."

This surprised the host, and he turned sharply to the colonel.

"What does that mean? What did you speak of?"

"Her charms were not entirely lost on me, Darcy. I am not a fool, you know." The colonel had moved his own plate to the side table. "Really, any man of good sense could not help admiring her. And I must confess that knowing you as a man of quite good sense, it does not entirely surprise me that you too were affected by those charms she has."

"But what did you *speak* of?"

"Reality, Darcy. Reality."

"I am in no mood for riddles, Richard. What do you mean?"

"Surely you know that you have luxuries that many a gentleman could not dream of. I admit enjoying the benefit of your largesse, as I conceded to Miss Elizabeth."

"But did you...did you suggest something *more*?"

"Oh, Darcy. *You* can be a fool. The reality is that she being somewhat poor in relative terms and me being...not rich and dependent on the drippings—I do not mean it unkindly and I say it without recrimination—of those who are."

"Such as me?"

"Such as you and perhaps somewhat Lady Catherine and even my father. No, the reality is that we both, Miss Elizabeth and I, knew that there was no possibility for the two of us."

"You spoke of such a thing?"

"We did not need to *speak* of it. But we both well understood it. That is all. It was a pleasant walk when we happened on each other. Indeed, I did what I could to bolster you to her. I was not so blind not to recognize *something* between the two of you while we were at Lady Catherine's pianoforte although, frankly, I think you both were and are too blind to have seen it."

"Bolster me?"

"I told her the story of you and that friend of yours, Bingley. How you came to his rescue. How it showed your true strength of character."

"Came to his rescue?"

"Darcy, you must stop repeating me. Yes, how he was tending towards a most inappropriate connection when you stepped in to preserve him. How could she not understand how well that reflected on your character? Too many think you devoted entirely to Fitzwilliam Darcy of Pemberley. I wanted her to know that you have true and genuine consideration for your friends.

"It is one of your great strengths, although you do try to hide it."

Darcy turned to the window. There. The wound felt regarding Jane was fresh in Miss Elizabeth's heart from his oblivious but well-meaning cousin. And he himself had twisted the knife! What he had done for Bingley *was* appropriate. He had no doubts about that, as he said in the letter he had written and given to her the morning after his disastrous offer. Now, at least, he understood how she knew of his intervention between Bingley and Jane.

The words from his cousin were cutting too deep. What happened was between him and her. He looked back at his friend.

"Thank you, Richard. In any case, for reasons I cannot share, she declined my offer, and I did not wish her to be uncomfortable with my continued presence at Rosings so I'm afraid I pressed you into fleeing with me."

"Well, Darcy. As a cavalryman, I will say it was a strategic retreat of the sort Wellington would have come up with. You will allow your wounds to heal and if she is that to you, you will develop your strategy and marshal your forces to make another effort to pierce her heart."

Darcy laughed at the attempted bravado as he turned back to look again out to Brook Street.

"Indeed," continued the colonel. "And now you stand at your fine window in your fine room after your own, devastating defeat."

He stood and approached his friend.

"I will leave it at that." He patted Darcy's shoulder. "Whatever I can do for you with that fine lady—and in the few days I have known her I understand her to be the sort of woman who would tempt any man—"

"Any man of good sense?"

"Indeed. Any such man, of which you truly are."

He touched Darcy on the shoulder a second time and with a wan smile removed himself to his room.

*   *   *   *

For his part, while back in town, the colonel regularly appeared at the War Office and even more at his regiment's club. But there was little to say or do with the peace having come. Events in America were droning on, but no further troops were thought necessary. With the end of the Peninsula War, a sizeable number of its veterans were shipped across the Atlantic, but it was felt that there was no need for more. He and his fellows were free to savor the hard-won peace and consider what was to become of them in what they hoped would be an extended period of peace.

As to the continent, matters had calmed since the downfall of Bonaparte, and England was content to see if the continentals could work matters out without the expenditure of more British blood or treasure.

These were thus pleasant days for the colonel as they were for Darcy (save for the lingering wound about which he could do nothing) and for his great friend Charles Bingley. The colonel thought Bingley a fine enough if in no way exceptional man and his lack of breeding—his wealth being the product of trade—was evident. This, too, was clear from his sisters, particularly the younger, insufferable, and unmarried one, a Miss Caroline Bingley. That she had her sights set on Darcy was evident from the first moment the colonel saw her when they were back in London after the abbreviated visit to Kent. He wondered whether his friend had disclosed the fact that his true love went in a far different direction. Darcy surely had not revealed that he had proposed to Elizabeth Bennet and been rejected. He doubted whether anyone but he and, perhaps, Bingley knew of *that*.

It was not for him, the colonel, to say anything, and he had not breached Darcy's confidence. Yet he was acutely aware that Darcy's attachment for the absent Miss

Bennet still consumed a part of him, however well he fought to keep it hidden. But they did not speak of it, or of her, again.

3

Colonel Fitzwilliam had enjoyed his cousin's hospitality in London for several weeks after they left Kent. He was also able to spend time with his brother's family in town. But it came to the time of the mass exodus, in his case to Haverford House in Lincolnshire. This was the Fitzwilliam family seat, situated some ten miles south of Lincoln, near the town of Waddington.

The estate itself was large, though not nearly as large as Pemberley, which stood some sixty miles to the northwest. The great house was, as the colonel himself told Elizabeth, built over time, and it reflected that, being a hodgepodge of a place with a core from the sixteenth century and wings added about every century or so thereafter. It was notoriously uncomfortable, especially in that ancient core. Several parts were closed off for large swathes of the year, to be opened only on the occasion of the visits by multitudes of guests.

But it had been some years since any such occasion occurred. The Earl, the Lord Waddington himself, had taken to remaining at the estate for the most part with the Countess Waddington. His eldest son and heir, Lord Ashworth, preferred London. This was not because he particularly reveled in society there. Instead, he had become quite a fine and talented amateur geologist since his days at Cambridge.

Lord Ashworth was part of a vibrant society in town and was a member of several Royal Societies. He also funded a number of foreign expeditions. What was most significant as far as his brother was concerned, though, was that he was married to the daughter of one of his Cambridge dons and that she had already borne him two sons (plus one daughter). In short, the colonel was slowly but inevitably dropping down in the chain of succession to the title and it was well that he had long since surrendered any hope let alone any expectation of acceding to it.

* * * *

Charles Bingley might have stayed in town, but he was convinced that a period in the north would do him good as well. He still rented an estate in Hertfordshire called Netherfield, some two miles from the village of Meryton, but he would rather be with his friend at Pemberley and so he and his sisters and his brother-in-law (Caroline Bingley and Mr. and Mrs. Hurst) joined Darcy and the colonel in the caravan to Derbyshire.

For her part, his sister Caroline would have preferred to return to Netherfield in Hertfordshire. This was not for any particular liking of the neighborhood, which she and her sister Mrs. Louisa Hurst found nearly intolerable what with families like the Bennets and the Lucases displaying such country manners and inappropriate airs. It was its proximity to town that would allow them to head back-and-forth as was their wont.

But especially with Fitzwilliam Darcy as the host, she was willing to suffer the interminable travel to the north and the isolation of Pemberley.

That settled, they all began the trek north and intermingled in the two chief carriages after most of the stops. When they reached Nottingham, the colonel separated from the others and headed east, for his family's estate in Lincolnshire, where he could spend needed time with his parents and have the opportunity to assess his situation in a now peaceful world and contemplate such domestic prospects as he might have.

He bid his *adieus* to the others. He rented the first in a series of horses he lightly rode east to his own family's seat outside of Waddington.

The solo ride was a great comfort to the colonel. He allowed his mount to dictate the pace and there was little traffic *en route*. He sat alone and content in the taverns along the way and again faced his own future. He was also at his leisure in reading. It was something he and many officers took up given the boredom of extended periods in Army camps. His tastes went to historical adventures and found *The Scottish Chiefs*, written by a woman of all people, particularly diverting.

As to what adventures lay in store for him in his future, he doubted there would be any. England had been at war virtually the entirety of his life. There was a brief peace in the years 2 and 3 but that could not and did not last. There had since been campaigns on land and on sea constantly ever since. Nelson had his great triumph at Trafalgar in 1805, and the Royal Navy controlled the seas, allowing ambitious captains to make their fortunes taking French prizes.

Colonel Fitzwilliam had his commission and was proud of it. He was proud of how he performed when he was brutally tested. He had only been a major when he first arrived in Portugal but now was a full colonel and safe at home with Bonaparte sitting in exile on Elba in the Med. His thoughts turned to what he was to do as a civilian which could not help but lead him to dwell on whether there could be any prospect of finding a suitable bride.

Once he had reached Haverford House, he was happy to be home with his father and mother, and he quickly was settled into his routine. He made sure to go for at least one ride, if not two, each day. He became again a familiar horseman around Waddington and the other nearby towns and villages, making a point of stopping at an inn or tavern for his midday meal almost every day.

He also made a point of visiting a number of nearby families, including families whose children he had grown up with and played with. At least once a week, he ventured into nearby Lincoln itself and stayed overnight several times after attending an entertainment in that city's emporium.

He was disappointed in one respect, however. Not a fortnight after arriving, he received a letter from Darcy. They had agreed that he would venture to visit Pemberley for several days, it not being much of a strain getting to and from that great house in Derbyshire.

Darcy's letter was somewhat cryptic, saying little more than that due to an unexpected change in circumstances, he was forced to return immediately to London. He wrote that he could not say for how long it would be but that there was some sort of transaction that needed to be resolved, though he gave no inkling of what that might be.

It was, although the colonel did not then know it, to do with the same Elizabeth Bennet who had so abruptly caused Darcy to change plans at Rosings Park many months earlier. While she and the Gardiners—Mr. Gardiner being her mother's brother—were enjoying a stroll on the grounds of Pemberley itself, as outsiders were permitted to do, she found herself suddenly and *very* unexpectedly face-to-face with the property's owner, who would be one equally startled Fitzwilliam Darcy. Which of the two was more discombobulated will never be known.

Soon after Elizabeth recovered from the shock of seeing him in his own home, a home she had so viciously (as she sometimes thought it to have been) rejected. And her antipathy towards the man began seeping away from her heart and she was introduced at her inn in Lambton to Georgiana Darcy and met Charles Bingley as well, the latter inquiring as to Jane Bennet's health and the condition of the rest of her family.

It was such a fine meeting that Elizabeth and the Gardiners were prevailed upon to visit Pemberley itself the next day, which they did and where Elizabeth had an uncomfortable reunion with Bingley's sisters.

It was not long after that, though, when everything was violently altered.

But in Lambton, Elizabeth received a pair of letters, sent days apart, from Jane. The earlier of those letters had been misdirected. That one expressed the family's concern about news regarding Lydia. The second letter brought confirmation of a most horrible turn of events, of George Wickham having run off with her little sister to an uncertain fate.

Elizabeth's despair over the news was worsened when she told it to Darcy, who had arrived just as she was receiving the news. He quickly disappeared from her and her life in a manner that was polite and no more, and she felt much the poorer for it.

Things happened very fast, and Elizabeth ended up hurrying back to Longbourn, where she found her mother in apoplexy and her father and uncle traveling to London trying valiantly to salvage at least some of the reputation of Lydia in particular and all the Bennets in general for her seduction by George Wickham. And somehow by the grace of God but more by the efforts of one Fitzwilliam Darcy, matters were largely put to rights when Lydia and Wickham married. They moved to Newcastle so that Wickham could join a regiment of infantry with a commission secretly paid for by Darcy himself.

Colonel Fitzwilliam knew none of this while he was in Lincolnshire, although he would later hear the story many times from many witnesses. All he knew was that Darcy had unexpectedly gone to London so that his own trip to Pemberley was jeopardized.

But Darcy's letter had a postscript that said that while most of the visitors would soon be heading back to town, Georgiana would remain and perhaps he should come to spend some time with her. He was on the road heading west the next day.

He had not given notice that he was coming, but Pemberley had long been like a second home to him, and he was greeted by Mrs. Reynolds, the housekeeper, with glee. The stablemaster could not wait to have him inspect the contents of the Pemberley stable of which he was justifiably proud with the discerning eye of a true cavalryman.

But nothing exceeded the enthusiasm of Georgiana herself. She insisted when she got word of the surprise arrival that he sit with her as soon as he was presentable and so began his weeklong stay in the height of country luxury.

They sat alone the first night for dinner, and both were pleased for the company. As courses were being changed, he asked her what she knew of her brother's sudden race to London.

"I cannot say for sure," she said as the meat course was being placed in front of her. "We had the most unusual visit by Miss Elizabeth Bennet and—"

"Elizabeth Bennet?" asked the colonel, with a sudden change of countenance. "The Elizabeth Bennet he met in Hertfordshire?"

For a moment, Georgiana was unnerved by the sudden change in her cousin's tone. She recovered. "I believe that is the one. I cannot imagine my brother knows more than one Elizabeth Bennet. Have you met her?"

Now, *she* was genuinely puzzled.

"I did. I was with your brother at your aunt's, Lady Catherine's, and we happened to meet her while she was visiting a family friend, who was married to the Hunsford parson." He paused to consider whether to say more but felt compelled to. "He told me afterwards that this Miss Bennet had a strange effect on him."

"On my brother?" She almost laughed at the absurdity but then recovered. "Well, I will admit that he did mention her several times to me as a woman of, what did he call it?, a formidable disposition and very fine eyes. Now that I think of it," she said, as the meat on both of their plates was going cold, "I think she might have had a quite unusual effect on him."

"A pleasant effect?" suggested the officer.

"Indeed. Though I cannot say, frankly, whether I am fit to judge since I see him so rarely and I have never seen my dear brother ever glanced by Cupid's arrow."

The colonel laughed and lifted his knife and fork to begin the course, and his cousin followed suit. They were largely silent at this point, but thoughts of Fitzwilliam Darcy and Elizabeth Bennet were foremost in both of their minds as they prattled on about gossip and memories and anything but Cupid and his arrow.

After dinner, the cousins adjourned to the drawing room. The colonel had poured himself a glass of port, and Georgiana was happy with a sherry.

After some hesitation, the colonel decide to ride straight in.

"What can you tell me about your brother and this Elizabeth Bennet?"

"After you left us in Nottingham," Georgiana said when she had collected her thoughts, "he rode ahead to see to some estate business with the steward. Charles Bingley thought to go, but Caroline insisted that he remain with us, and so he did. My brother got a sole horse the last morning and rode it and I imagine a replacement horse to get to the house."

She continued. "I cannot imagine what he encountered when he got here. At dinner the evening when the rest of them arrived, though, he did mention that he had come across Miss Bennet, visiting the house with her aunt and her uncle. Now that I think on it, Caroline Bingley seemed to go a bit pale when he said this, though with her fair skin it is not so easy to tell."

This was of a good deal of interest to the colonel, who had been long starved of civilian tattle.

"In any case, he began talking about how fine a woman this Elizabeth Bennet was and he got downright cross when Miss Bingley said she was perhaps 'passable as a country girl but not more.'

"He glared at her with a glare I am glad he directed in my direction only occasionally."

"Well, you were a fairly well-behaved girl all in all," the colonel said.

"I was, yes. In any case, it was enough to silence her and the rest of the table as he exchanged comments about her with Charles Bingley, who had met her when he had a house near where the Bennets live."

"That is what I'm led to understand, too. It is the country house that Bingley rented."

"He made this Miss Bennet sound like a likeable enough creature, so I asked whether I might meet her. 'I cannot say how long she will be in Lambton,' he said, 'since she had was just on a passing visit with her aunt and uncle from town,' to which Caroline could not resist saying that her uncle was in trade, which even her sister thought was quite beyond the pale, giving her an 'oh,

Caroline,' and my brother ignored this and said that he would go into Lambton early the next day and would bring me to meet her, which we did, with something of a pleasant reunion with Bingley.

"She then came to the house and I must say things were very cold with Caroline Bingley. She promised to come again and I was very much looking forward to that. Sadly, when my brother went to see her in Lambton that morning, she had just received some troubling news and was forced to head up to town without delay."

During the course of this recital, the colonel had moved to the front of his chair and this prompted Georgiana to ask if he would like more tea, but he declined. He would not have her interrupt her story for a moment and after the brief pause and after she had taken a sip of her own tea to steady herself, she resumed.

"He was very distraught," she said, "and I, of course, was very disappointed, but he would not say what it was about. Instead, he came back to the house with us and before anyone knew it, he was off on his way, alone, to town. I do not know what he said to Bingley, but the rest of them were running around packing and such and the next morning were gone back to town themselves, leaving me here and now so grateful for your coming to visit."

The colonel knew something was bubbling but could not fathom what it was. He would not imagine Darcy had tried another proposal, but that must be a possibility. He found he enjoyed Georgiana's company. She was alone in the great house with several tutors from whom she still took lessons. She was proficient in all the skills some think an accomplished woman ought to have. Her French was good, but her Italian was just passable (though the colonel had the capacity for neither). She and her tutors had long since accepted that at best she had become adequate in Greek and Latin, and she had come to relish that this particular shortcoming absolved her of having to delve into the ancients.

Her greatest accomplishment, though, was at the pianoforte. The colonel had heard references to this long before, on the trip to Rosings Park when he met Elizabeth Bennet, the trip on which Lady Catherine seemed to have acquired a thesaurus of insults to fling at the innocent Bennet girl, not understanding that the gallant Fitzwilliam Darcy easily and naturally stepped into the role of her guardian.

Of course both the colonel and Darcy were Georgiana's guardians, an obligation accepted with the utmost seriousness. The colonel was some ten years older than she was and the age and the life experience and the nearly filial obligations could mean nothing to either of them than the most cherished one of close family members.

So the colonel enjoyed Georgiana's company at Pemberley as a true, if older, friend, both of them glad not to be on their own in the country.

He extended his stay to a fortnight, but at last it was time to return to Lincolnshire and his parents. They had seen relatively little of him during his service on the Peninsula and elsewhere, so he committed to remain at least through the Christmas holidays and his brother had promised to make the trip north with his own family into the new year.

That commitment, though, was tested when several weeks after he was back at Haverford House following that extended stay at Pemberley, he received the most remarkable letter.

Brook Street

November 22, 1814

Richard,

Though you will be shocked, I daresay, to hear my most pleasant news, your reaction will be nothing compared to my own. For, you see, Miss Elizabeth Bennet has consented to become Mrs. Fitzwilliam Darcy.

The colonel found this news quite interesting. He had discovered the letter when he had returned from a ride. It sat on a silver tray on a table in the foyer. He recognized Darcy's hand and carried it to the sitting room and after receiving some coffee from a footman, sat in a favorite chair and before he could take a sip read:

I know you will consider me the luckiest of men seeing as you have met, though all too briefly as I recall you saying, Miss Bennet. And I must acknowledge that you have been proved right in your assurance that my retreat from Rosings Park after my first attempt at seizing that woman's heart was most likely a strategic one as part of a far longer campaign. And I, sir, have proved victorious.

I have not kept you informed of my goings on since you left us in Nottingham to go to Haverford House as we continued to Pemberley. I take full responsibility for that lapse and hope you will forgive me. I believe Georgiana may have told you some things but it is hardly the full story. When we spoke about the fact that Miss Elizabeth had rejected my initial, so ill-delivered offer, I did not explain her reasons. There were more than I would like to admit concerning my own defects—as she then saw them—but her specific attention was on *two points. One concerned my own failure to allow my friend Charles Bingley to become aware that Miss Elizabeth's sister was in fact in London when he was. I insisted to her that I did so as a matter of friendship. On one of your turns with her, though, you characterized it as something of a triumph for me. You were not to know that when you spoke to her of saving my friend from an imprudent connection you were talking about her own family. Instead of crediting me for what I had done, <u>she condemned me for it</u>.*

I told her at the time that I believed my actions were justified. I have come to understand that I was mistaken in my motive and have duly apologized to her as well as her sister Jane and Bingley and attempted to atone for it, which, you will understand, I have managed to do with some success.

The second reason she gave for rejecting me at first is one with which you will be familiar. George Wickham. She felt I treated him most deplorably when, she thought, I arbitrarily denied him the living my father expected he would have. You know the truth about that and about the incident with Georgiana that I will not repeat but that I felt I must tell Miss Elizabeth about so she might appreciate the true nature of George Wickham's character.

I did this in a letter I handed to her on the day before we left Rosings Park.

The colonel recalled that letter well and was pleased to have at last learned its contents, though he was not so sure about the appropriateness of Darcy having disclosed what he had disclosed about Georgiana. Still, there was nothing to be done about that and he doubted that it would come to anything given how Darcy and Elizabeth had ended up as they had ended up.

He continued his reading.

I did not see Miss Elizabeth after we left Rosings Park for many months. I could not, though, alter my feelings towards her, much as I struggled to do. I was resigned to having lost the one woman with whom I felt tremendous admiration and affection and, more, love.

Life continued for me while you were in my company and I should have perhaps resigned myself to marrying our cousin Anne as Lady Catherine wished so greatly that I would had not perhaps the work of Providence intervened. By which I mean, through the most extraordinary of coincidences, I found myself face to face with the same Miss Elizabeth Bennet on the grounds of Pemberley itself! I had only shortly before decided to hurry to the estate to address some issues with my steward and she happened to be nearby and, based upon the assurance that no one in the family would be present, visited with her aunt and uncle, the latter a man of trade living in Cheapside.

To them, it was merely another great house to tour on their trip to Derbyshire, but it turned out to be much more, at least to Elizabeth and me.

I go on too long. Suffice it to say that in time Elizabeth told me that her view of me had modified much in my favour since she had resisted my advances the first time. My feelings towards her had not changed, and somehow she agreed to become my wife.

The wedding will be at the Bennets' church in Meryton, and you will attend. Or so that is my great request. My bride and I, with perhaps Mr. and Mrs. Bingley (who are going to be married with us), will be traveling to Pemberley for our wedding trip.

Yours, &c., &c,
Fitzwilliam Darcy

The devil, you, the colonel told himself. He was naturally surprised by these tidings from his cousin and was quite excited that Miss Elizabeth Bennet would be formally joining his family in some slight way.

$$4.$$

It must be said that before this letter was dispatched from London, Darcy had gone with Elizabeth to Longbourn, the first order being obtaining Mr. Bennet's consent to the match. He had already and quite readily given his consent to Bingley marrying Jane. But that was Jane and Bingley and this was his dearest Lizzy and the standoffish Darcy. Consent followed, though, when Lizzy vouched for Darcy's true character and especially when she insisted that she truly loved the man.

Thus word spread quickly at Longbourn. Thanks to Mrs. Bennet's eagerness notwithstanding the unpleasantness of the groom to tell her sister and Mrs. Long and Lady Lucas and whoever else's ear she could latch onto.

Jane was there, too, aware before they arrived of Lizzy's intentions. While their mother was spreading the news and Jane was napping and Darcy and Bingley were riding, Kitty approached Lizzy.

Some months before, soon after Lydia had gone to Newcastle as Mrs. Wickham, Kitty had appealed first to Jane about joining her, but Jane had no influence on their father in such matters. Only Lizzy did, so Kitty appealed to her. Unfortunately (or so she at first thought) for Kitty, Lizzy was in complete agreement with her father. Indeed, though Kitty did not know this, it was Lizzy who made the greatest objections earlier about Lydia going to Brighton, and her fears had been too sadly realized.

"No," she had told Kitty, "I cannot and will not suggest to Papa that you go to the north. It will be the ruination of you, no matter how many husbands Lydia thinks she can find for you."

Which only succeeded in enhancing Kitty's sulk and extending the period of time she sat alone doing no one knew what in her room, the one she had long shared with Lydia, whose absence only deepened her outrage.

But that was long before and now Kitty faced a different crisis when Jane and Lizzy themselves left Longbourn.

Which is why when Jane was out, she knocked on Lizzy's door. Her attitude was worlds apart than in that earlier episode.

Lizzy stood to see what her sister wanted. After taking a deep breath, Kitty began.

"When you and Jane are gone, you must take me with you."

Lizzy had not considered this given all of the other things that had to be taken care of related to her and Jane's weddings.

"I do not understand," she said as she directed Kitty to sit beside her on the side of the bed.

"I just cannot stay here with Mamma and Mary. Papa is always in his library and does not come out. Mamma keeps telling me I will never find a husband after I had my chance when the militia was here and Lydia found her Wickham. And Mary is just Mary and even worse since I'm the only one she can lecture to.

"I hate it here, Lizzy. I now understand why I could not go to Newcastle. But, now, can I go with you and Darcy?"

Lizzy considered what was being asked of her. She knew that she would not wish to be left at the house when the others had left. So she was sympathetic. She whispered, "I will speak to our father about it first and if he approves I will speak to Darcy." She backed from Kitty, who turned and blinked several times and asked, "Promise?"

"Promise," Lizzy assured her.

"I think Papa will be happy to be rid of me, as long as it's not to Newcastle."

"You must understand why he did not allow you to go. He did not wish you to end up like Lydia."

"What's wrong with Lydia?" Kitty seemed genuinely puzzled.

"If you do not understand that, I have little hope for you."

"I'm sorry. I am not so simple as I guess she is and as I was. I cannot see myself throwing myself at a soldier. I think I am past that at least."

"You had better be," Lizzy said. "If you are to come to town, things will be quite different, and I think you will be very much happier. But I will first speak to Papa and then to Darcy."

Elizabeth sat with her father that very day, in his library. He was quickly in agreement. "I would not dream of her wandering about the world if I did not have your assurance that you will be watchful of her. And I have that assurance, do I not?"

"Of course, Papa. You know I will see to her."

"Well, Lizzy, if anyone can do it, you can."

With her father's consent in hand, which Kitty was glad to hear. Lizzy sat with Darcy, as she had promised.

And when she did, he did not react well, which confused his wife who thought he had left his first impressions of her family behind.

"Kitty? My God, Elizabeth, she was as bad as the other one. Running around like a spoiled child, and from what you say it does not appear that she has changed in the slightest. Live with us? Absolutely not."

The two were strolling alone in Meryton.

"My dear," Lizzy responded, "I think she was too attached to Lydia, though she is older. She let Lydia lead her about. She is a good girl, I think, but too easily swayed. I think I can make something of her. I really do. If she becomes too disruptive, we can always send her back to Longbourn. But we can give her a taste of city life and encourage her to grow into the woman I believe she can grow into and perhaps find herself a suitable husband."

"Unlike the scoundrel her sister found."

Lizzy shook her head and gave him a slight tug of censure. "Wickham will, I believe, make Lydia happy."

"Whether she can make him happy is another thing altogether, but I think it best if we refrain from speaking of that...officer as much as possible."

"I am not endorsing him. You know that. But you are right in a sense, and I think it bolsters Kitty's argument to be kept as far from him and his like as possible. I'm afraid she cannot last long alone with my mother and Mary and even my father in Longbourn."

"So we must take her in?" asked Darcy, in resignation.

"I think we must, but you must be more willing to be open about her. I will be chiefly with her, but you must promise me that you will be civil."

"I am always civil."

"Darcy. You were barely civil to me when we met, if you will recall."

He smiled, though she did not see it. Their growing affection for one another had not tempered certain of her memories of him.

"Very well. I will try to be particularly civil to her. Can she not stay with Jane?"

"She will of course see Jane frequently, but we all know that if Kitty is to be put right, the tasks falls to me and I will accept the challenge."

"You may tell her, then, that she is welcome to come to Brook Street when we return from the country as husband and wife."

"I think Georgiana will also be a help with her. They are near the same age."

He paused. "You do have a point, my dear. Yes, that is definitely worth considering. I hope that your sister will become quite a friend to my sister."

"It is settled then." They continued their walk, now turning back towards Longbourn.

"Why do I feel you are always manipulating me in some ways?" Darcy asked.

"I am only leading you to understand what you want to understand."

"Yes, my dear. I believe that is it," and they continued their walk speaking of other matters related to the wedding until they returned to the Bennets'.

*   *   *   *

Late in the afternoon on the penultimate day in Longbourn, Lizzy was lying down in her room. Jane was off in Meryton with her mother and her aunt.

There was a slight knock on the door. Lizzy pushed herself to her elbows. She had not been asleep. She was enjoying the quiet of the country noises that she long enjoyed as they cascaded over the fields that surrounded the house.

"Come in," she called. She was completely taken aback by who should enter. It was Mary. If she had crossed the room's threshold five times in recent years it would be a lot. Now she stood close to the door, coiled in a position with which Lizzy was also unfamiliar.

"Mary?" said Lizzy as she began to rise from the bed.

"May I come in?" her sister asked, and after a "please" from Lizzy, she closed the door and moved to the bed, joining Lizzy on its side.

"I know that Kitty has spoken to you," she said, and Lizzy said that she had.

Mary reached for her sister's hands. They looked at one another in a way that they never had before. Even sisterly.

"I do not want to be left here. I know she thinks she will be leaving to go with you when you marry Mr. Darcy. I must do something to...to get away."

"Mary, you will be here with mother and father."

"That's just it. I will be here with mother and father and only with Momma and Papa."

As had happened with Kitty, Elizabeth told her she would consider the alternatives to this. The clear one was that she go to Jane. She doubted that either of their parents would be particularly troubled by Mary's leaving Longbourn. Neither of them cared for who was plainly the least of their daughters and who likely dove into the alternatives that she had dived into as a sanctimonious nag in part because she was neither Jane nor Lizzy and she was neither Kitty nor Lydia.

When she next was alone with Jane, then, Elizabeth raised the prospect of Mary's moving in with the Bingleys'. And, bless them, they both agreed that it was something of an obligation that Jane was bound to undertake seeing as Elizabeth had accepted Kitty as *her* guest.

For her part, Mary thought going with Jane and Charles was the best chance for her, particularly to be able to socialize with and attend seminars and symposia with like-minded theologians—as she considered herself—in the otherwise Gomorrahian world that she wholly expected London to be.

5.

Before the weddings themselves, as preparations were being made, visits to both Brook Street and Meryton were frequent. Elizabeth decided to take advantage of the proximities to have Kitty and Georgiana spend time together.

Netherfield had been reopened for the wedding, providing accommodation for those coming from London. Bingley's sisters immediately made themselves at home in the bedchambers they had occupied in their initial visit, with Caroline resuming the role of the *de facto* mistress of the house.

The ceremonies themselves were simple enough country affairs. In fact, it was unusual in that the Darcys' wedding took place with the wedding between Elizabeth's older sister Jane and Darcy's great friend Charles Bingley. The colonel was pleased to have been forgiven by all the interested parties for whatever clumsy role he unknowingly played in the relationship between those latter two, save in a bizarre fashion by Caroline Bingley who got into her head that the colonel had managed to push Darcy closer to Eliza Bennet with his *faux pas* about the scheme to keep Charles and Jane apart.

That was neither here nor there for the colonel, who managed to avoid exchanging a single word with Bingley's unmarried sister beyond a perfunctory introduction the night before the wedding.

Which was neither here nor there for that lady, seeing as the colonel was hardly rich or handsome enough to tempt her.

The colonel had had a delightful time on the carriage journey down from Derbyshire with Georgiana, riding easily in the chill late autumn air to London. The cousins would both be staying at her brother's house on Brook Street until traveling to Meryton the day before the wedding. A party was held that night at Netherfield. And so, both the colonel and his cousin Georgiana at last met Elizabeth's parents and her sisters Jane, Mary, and Kitty.

As for Lydia, she remained with her husband, the execrable Captain Wickham, outside of Newcastle and said she could not be spared from her obligations to him, and he could not be spared from his obligations to the Army.

The colonel was pleased to be introduced to Mr. and Mrs. Gardiner, Elizabeth's aunt and uncle from Cheapside who had been with her on that fateful day at Pemberley. At one point, the colonel sat for a very enjoyable quarter of an hour discussing all manner of things with Mr. Gardiner, who he found intelligent and very respectable.

That was perhaps the longest conversation he had among the guests as the wedding ceremony was brief and the parties dispersed soon after a wedding breakfast at the Meryton Assembly. After which Mr. and Mrs. Darcy and Mr. and Mrs. Bingley left in a pair of carriages with Georgiana to go together to Derbyshire to spend the Christmas season and the early part of the year 15 at Pemberley.

The colonel arranged for a carriage to take him to London, sitting awkwardly with Mr. and Mrs. Hurst and Caroline Bingley, for the duration until they separated when he stopped at his brother's while they continued to Grosvenor Square.

That business done, in two days' time, he and his brother's family somehow fit themselves into a carriage for the seasonal trip to Waddington.

6.

The colonel very much enjoyed his time with the entirety of the Fitzwilliam clan in Lincolnshire. It was too long since he had had the chance to see his nephews and niece, and the three seemed to have grown remarkably.

The children also seemed to cause his parents to revert to their own childhoods in insisting on playing with the actual children.

He always found his sister-in-law a most pleasant creature, well-educated growing up in Cambridge and lacking, bless her, in some of the superficial characteristics too often encountered in a woman in society, especially one in town.

The group took in entertainments in Lincoln several times and especially those related to the season.

In time, though, even the novelty of being in the country with its cold air and bits of snow wore off and the children were anxious to return to their home in Mayfair. In truth, so were their parents and so after a small ball held by the Earl and Countess after the new year arrived, Lord and Lady Ashworth and their three children made themselves as comfortable and warm as they could be made and began the journey south to London.

Alone again with his parents, the colonel rode when he could, keeping his horses safely in their stalls when the weather was too cold and the footing on the trails and highways was frozen too rough and potted to be safe for their hooves. He also spent his time taking advantage of his father's library. It was nearly the equal of the one at Pemberley, but it was well complete enough for him to bury himself into some work of fiction as he had in similarly long and lonely stretches of his life as a boy, often with his brother cloistered in a corner of the room with a collection of the scientific tracts in which he was so interested.

7.

It was a cold winter in Derbyshire and neither of the brides was accustomed to it. The several times they were required to remain in the great house at Pemberley, not even able to go for a stroll and with their husbands unable to go for a ride for the accumulated snow.

At least the pantries were well stocked and there was enough wood to keep the fires burning and enough of the freshness of the early months of marriage to allow Mr. and Mrs. Darcy and Mr. and Mrs. Bingley to be in their own worlds of happiness and contentment.

By mid-January, though, they agreed that it was time to return to London. On the first of February, after a period of fine and warm (or at least warmer) weather that left the roads clear, the two couples and Georgiana began the days' long journey. They arrived four days later to their houses in Mayfair and were quickly warming themselves by the fires that had been set in anticipation of their arrivals.

The very moment she had settled herself, even before checking the household accounts, Mrs. Darcy sat down at the fine, feminine desk in her new study in her new home. She removed a sheet of heavy, cream-colored stationery from a drawer and cut a fine pen that she dipped into a brass inkwell on that desk and invited Kitty to join her, her husband, and her new sister-in-law to London.

She placed her new seal on it and then pulled a cord and upon the appearance of a young footman whose name Lizzy promised herself she would remember stepped from her desk and handed it to him with instructions that it promptly be dispatched to Longbourn, which it was.

With no sign of snow in London, the next day found Lizzy, Jane, and Georgiana strolling in Hyde Park and Darcy and Bingley getting some exercise on horses on the trails there as well.

Since in her letter to Kitty, Lizzy said she and Jane would collect her and Mary at Longbourn two days later, e Early on the day after this walk, Jane and Elizabeth sat in a Darcy barouche for the trip north. They arrived shortly before midday, the roads and the weather being favorable.

After a meal among all the Bennets excepting Lydia, goodbyes were said and assurance of many future visits were given, and trunks being loaded, the sisters headed back to town where they were all anxious about embarking on their new lives.

The friendship between Kitty and Georgiana that was hinted at when they were together around Meryton for the wedding did quite well in the great metropolis. Their bedchambers were beside one another on the Brook Street house's second floor and much as Kitty and Lydia were nearly inseparable in the long-ago days at Longbourn, so became the case for these two in London.

Neither had spent much time in the city apart from a brief period when Georgiana was under the tutelage of a Mrs. Younge before the near tragedy of a forced elopement with Wickham. As to that, few knew of it and Kitty was not among them. Only Darcy and Elizabeth at the house and Colonel Fitzwilliam, who was still up in Lincolnshire. And Georgiana, but she had not breathed a word of the shameful episode to a soul.

This in part explained why Kitty and Georgiana did not have as much independence alone as they might have liked when they went for their strolls since Elizabeth insisted that a Darcy footman keep near them to avoid the not unrealistic danger of them being kidnapped. Still, it was as close to independence as ladies such as them, especially one such as Georgiana with a large fortune for the taking, could expect.

8.

The calmness abruptly snapped after word reached London in early March 1815 that Napoleon Bonaparte had fled his exile on the Mediterranean island of Elba and was likely heading to Paris. By late that month, this information had spread throughout Britain. The colonel was at Haverford House when he heard but could do nothing until he received orders explaining where he was to travel to collect and prepare his men for the trip to the continent. The next morning, a rider raced to the door at the house, banging harshly with an urgent message for the colonel. When he had seen the rider approach, he had hurried to the foyer and received the message immediately from the butler.

Norwich.

He was to arrive with all dispatch to an encampment that was being established to the southeast of Norwich in Norfolk County. The colonel knew the town. It was close to the North Sea and had a port that could handle the demands of a number of army regiments for transport to France or Holland or wherever they were needed.

It would be a long ride, but he was soon taking it, his travel bags being readied immediately after news of Bonaparte's reappearance reached him. He said his goodbyes to his parents, both of whom were more anxious about his going, especially his father, than he expected.

Because of his need to keep his own mount for whatever was to happen, he rode only him to the first exchange spot and arranged for a rider to take him the rest of the way at a pace that was too relaxed for the colonel himself. Instead, he rode hard and exchanged horses frequently. On the second day after a night spent at an inn midway, he met several other cavalrymen heading to Norwich, and they rode as a group, resplendent in their red and green and blue coats and with their swords and scabbards dangling from their sides and cheered on in every town, village, and hamlet they went through along the way. He arrived on the third day since he left Haverford House.

*　*　*　*

As the officers and troopers settled in, dispatches crossed the Channel each day. Fast horses were arranged along the route from Dover to London so that the latest news would not be delayed any more than geography required. And that news was not good. The colonel and the other officers and the ministers were increasingly shocked at Bonaparte's progress. Worse, it was soon clear that there were few Frenchmen who would oppose him. To the contrary, the hard realization was that the deposed "Emperor" would be able to raise an army that would rival that of Britain, Prussia, and their allies.

In response to the increasing threat, the four allies each agreed to field an army of 150,000 men. The British officers, though, well knew that the best of their troops had been sent to America when the view was that war on the continent was finally over for good. It now appeared to have been a short-lived victory. They had to rebuild an army of troops far less enthusiastic than were the other side's, who were vying to be included in the French Corps.

The colonel's cavalry regiment, the 1st Royal Dragoons, was greatly in need of cavalrymen. They had the benefit of their troops not being such ruffians as were often pressed to fill out the regiments of infantry—such as George Wickham's—and artillery, it being necessary that each man have a deep familiarity with riding and controlling their mounts. The core of the officers and non-commissioned officers from the Peninsula were in camps that sprung up throughout England, chiefly the south or east where there was ready access to the Channel or the North Sea and thus to the continent.

For the colonel's regiment, many of his fellow officers had personal horses that were qualified for war duty, as was the colonel's Atlas, and those horses arrived, to be mixed in with the horses owned and trained by the Army itself.

9.

In Norwich, there was precious little time to do anything but train and go through what information came from the War Office with the higher officers of the various regiments that were clustered together.

On a clear morning shortly after arriving, angry shouts floated into the colonel's tent, followed by the personage of the colonel's aide, Major Michael Groeper, himself.

"They are joining him!" was what was being said again and again, and in a moment the major was upon the colonel, slightly out of breath.

"It is true, sir. We've received an official dispatch from London. Bonaparte is not being stopped by the French who were left in charge. They are following him! They will follow him to hell, apparently. That is all they and we know. They cannot say what it does and will mean, sir, but it has created quite a crisis, I must tell you."

The colonel was on his feet before the major had finished this. The two made their way through the camp's makeshift streets and the crowd of men and officers that had gathered in the foyer and outside the old regimental headquarters, joined by a flow of other officers pushing their way towards the main hall where they assembled as a group to receive their orders.

As he got near, the colonel heard General Ponsonby's voice cutting through, saying that he knew nothing more than they did. When the officers had got themselves into some sort of order, the general stood on the dais and spoke to the standing men. Yes, he said, he had received an urgent dispatch from the War Office. Yes, it said that it was clear that Bonaparte would have to be stopped by the allies as the French were unwilling to take him on.

Worse, as the first rumors had it, they were joining him, the fools. Joining the tyrant and throwing the world back to war and chaos.

"Beyond that, gentlemen, we know nothing. We can only—we *must* only—assume the worst. The War Office and Whitehall are monitoring this very carefully, but it is my view that we have no alternative, gentlemen, to preparing ourselves to resume that hateful war though, God willing, we will be able to put an end to him once and for all this time even if the diplomats have proved themselves incapable of doing their job."

This speech was interrupted several times by huzzahs from the officers and men who had filled the room. When the general was done, the more senior officers, Colonel Fitzwilliam among them, followed him out to the palatial office that was the center of the various regiments under his command.

When they were there and silence reigned, the general repeated that he knew no more than what he had told them. He ordered them, though, to prepare their regiments as if they would sail "at a moment's notice" for the continent.

"You will understand, gentlemen, that from this moment we must do nothing but prepare our men. We are a bit soft in some areas with this illusionary peace that I admit I was perhaps too optimistic would be preserved and we must redouble our efforts to get to full strength. We will let the diplomats and the War Office undertake to bring our allies back together but that will take some time. For now, please sit with your officers to plan what we are to do. Pray God we have heard this soon enough to prepare ourselves."

With that and murmurs among the officers, they all left to go to the offices for each of the individual regiments. When the colonel reached the one for the 1st

Royal Dragoons, Major Groeper, a pair of captains, and several other lower officers as well as his top non-commissioned officers were crowded into the room.

When everyone was sitting or standing as was their wont, the colonel merely repeated what he had been told, and the group commenced discussing how they would get the regiment into fighting trim.

In the days and weeks that followed with constantly changing weather, regular dispatches were received from London.

Things were progressing in a most unsatisfactory way. Bonaparte had reached Paris and the King was gone. War was inevitable.

As it happened, a day or two after Colonel Fitzwilliam had joined his dragoons outside of Norwich, Captain George Wickham's Infantry Regiment was aboard a number of transports. Under the protection of several ships of the Royal Navy, the convoy of Elizabeth Bennet's brother-in-law headed south from Newcastle directly to the Low Countries, where their training for the upcoming battles would resume.

Wickham had joined the regiment Darcy had gotten him into only a few months before it received its orders to head to the continent. It was quite a shock to Lydia, who had no real expectation or understanding that her husband would be leaving her so soon and for an uncertain fate, perhaps even to fight in anger.

She immediately wrote to her parents. They were somewhat anxious about what would happen to their son-in-law in light of Bonaparte's reemergence, and things were made worse when they received Lydia's letter confirming their fears: Wickham would be gone to war. Hence Lydia needed to be with her family, her husband having none.

Of course, she was told by her father in his response, she must return to Longbourn. They could not know what the fates held in store for her husband, the captain, he said, but she belonged with her own family while she waited.

"Your mother is most anxious that you shall 'return to my bosom,' she has said and so you must make it so. We await your arrival by the fastest means possible and you shall be most welcome to be with us again."

These were sentiments that did not quite reflect Mr. Bennet's own view of the matter, but it was plain that Lydia would return home while Wickham was away at war and his obligation as her father was to welcome her when she did.

Though when Lydia did arrive, her mother was disappointed in one respect. Her daughter was not yet with child.

*   *   *   *

Lydia found it the easiest of things to dip into the role of the officer's young wife at Longbourn. Two or three days after her arrival, she was comfortably in a chair in the sitting room.

"Will he only be a captain when it is over?" Maria Lucas asked, in quite a state of excitement while she sat with her mother and Lydia, with Sir William moving about the room and interjecting appropriate compliments about Captain Wickham and the sacrifices he and his bride were making for the country.

"My one regret," Lydia said amid the enthusiasm, "is that he has yet to put me in the family way."

"Not for want of trying," Maria said as she clapped her hands.

To this, Lydia simply smiled, assuring the girl with a giggle that she was spot on in her assessment.

But Longbourn was too quiet. Lydia soon tired of the scant company that Meryton had to offer. Her temperament was not aided by the loss of the attention from officers she had come to enjoy and expect in Newcastle, especially after the four-and-twenty families that her mother was forever claiming were on intimate terms with the Bennets no longer paid particular attention to the soldier's—officer's—wife. She had become accustomed to being the object of many an officer's attention.

Within the week of appearing at the Bennet family estate, Lydia wrote to Kitty at Brook Street. The two had not seen each other once after Lydia was off with her husband to the north.

Now, though, Lydia insisted that she could not bear to have to spend a moment longer than absolutely necessary away from her dearest relation. "You must come," she wrote in her ungainly hand. "I shall suffer terribly if I am forced to be alone while my dearest Wickham is confronting the Frogs!"

Catherine—*her journey to London solidified her transformation from the childish name she had come to resent. Thus, dear reader, she will henceforth be known by her Christian name*—showed the letter to Elizabeth.

"I suppose you must go to her and her parents," the elder sister said, much to her sister's disappointment.

This was when they were sitting in the period before dinner on the day Lydia's plea arrived. She reached over to grasp Catherine's hands.

"I know you would prefer to be here—"

"Longbourn has become so foreign to me, Lizzy." Indeed, the sisters had ventured to Longbourn only about once a month, though it was not more than several hours ride away. And much as Lizzy enjoyed sitting in her father's library for a period when they arrived, Catherine was left to entertain a mother who continued to view this and all her other daughters as somehow lesser than her final one, the one lost to the north for she knew not how long.

Now, though, that daughter was back, and for Catherine this meant even less attention directed her way.

But Lizzy was right. Catherine supposed she must go. Thus, on the following Monday, the four London Bennets boarded a Darcy carriage for the ride to Hertfordshire. They arrived early enough to share the midday meal with their parents and Lydia. As the day was short, they could not venture a stroll through Meryton, it also being chilled, and the three eldest Bennets returned to town, leaving Catherine to her fate.

*　　*　　*　　*

As for the 1st Royal Dragoons and the other regiments that made up the "Union Brigade"—being from Scotland and Ireland as well as England—they did well in rebuilding their numbers and the cavalrymen were in good trim when the orders arrived for their departure to the Flemish port of Ostend.

Nervousness was widespread even amongst these seasoned cavalrymen and they were anxious to finish the trip. By late May, their transports had delivered them in Ostend and they rode to encampments not far from Brussels. From there, they could be positioned as the Duke of Wellington wished them to be for the expected and inevitable confrontation with a French army laden with hardened veterans.

In early June, the armies were moving around like pieces on a chessboard. Bonaparte testing and teasing and being tested and teased by Wellington and the

Prussian Blücher until the armies began to converge outside Brussels, near the town of Waterloo.

By mid-June, the inevitability of the battle hung heavy over each soldier and each horse in each of the encampments, Allied or French.

And in all those encampments, soldiers and officers sat in small groups with one another, trying as best they could to stay out of the rain, making promises. *You will go to my parents', eh?* many would ask. *You'll tell me wife I loves her?* Those who could write would set some however inadequate words down and fold the paper. Those who could not write would find someone who could to set those words down, and in certain of the squads, on all sides, scriveners were kept occupied for hours at a time, blessed to be diverted from their own anxiousness.

Before the battle, these *final words* would be collected and placed in the care of their colonel, to be returned should the soldier live to fight another day and to be delivered by an aide if the soldier did not.

Officers, too, though they had fancier paper and actual envelopes to be sealed. And so it was with Colonel Fitzwilliam and Major Groeper.

And they had a version of the conversation that echoed throughout.

"If I die," the colonel said, "you must promise me one thing. And do not tell me I will not die. We are both warriors and we are seeing death all around us so do not patronize me by suggesting otherwise."

"Understood."

"If I die, I have one task I need you to perform. As a friend and not as a subordinate. In a hidden pocket in my trunk, which I hope you will be able to get, there is a letter. It is addressed to and is to be given to my cousin, Fitzwilliam Darcy. You must promise to send my letter to him should I perish and to no one else. Do you understand?"

After a pause, the major nodded. "Yes. I understand, sir."

"Knowing that will be a comfort, although I hope it never comes to that."

And the major extracted a promise from the colonel that should *he* perish, the colonel would visit the major's parents in Cheapside. He would be in his uniform. And he would sit with Mr. and Mrs. Groeper and say what he could truthfully say about their brave son, should he not be able to ever sit with them again.

10.

Colonel Richard Fitzwilliam was brutally awakened he knew not when by the screaming. It was like a non-ending chorus of banshees all about him. He could not say whether it was day or night as his eyes were covered. His left leg throbbed horribly and incessantly, and a crest of pain engulfed him. He could not know whether his own screams had joined the others.

"Colonel Fitzwilliam."

The voice sounded familiar.

"It is Major Groeper, sir."

"Groeper?" The voice calmed him.

"Yes, sir. I have been...waiting for you to wake up."

"What became of us?"

"The Army?"

"Yes the Army you damn fool. What—?"

"It was a near run thing, sir, but in the end, it was Blücher and the Prussians who saved the day. We have won, sir, and Bonaparte is surely done for."

Into the darkness, the colonel said "Thank God" very quietly.

"Sir. Let me fetch the surgeon, sir. He told me to get him when you awoke."

"Groeper. Wait. I need some water. What time is it?"

"It is not long before dawn on Monday, sir."

The officer rushed to get a canteen, and when he returned with it, he opened it and held it so that his colonel could get some, but not too much, into his parched mouth. When the colonel nodded, the major pulled it away and put the stopper back in. "Now I must get the surgeon," he said.

Monday. And victory. So it was worth it in the end. Thank God.

It did not seem long to the colonel when Groeper returned.

"Colonel, this is Mr. Reynolds, sir. The surgeon."

"And how are you this morning, Colonel?" He placed a hand on the officer's right arm.

"Having heard of the victory, I am quite elated."

Though there was the constant drone of men in agony, something in the surgeon's voice and manner of speaking made his words sound crystal clear to his patient. "I expect you are. But how are *you*?"

"I cannot see, and my left leg is giving me all manner of trouble. But I believe it is for *you* to tell how I really am."

He heard the doctor pull up and sit on a chair.

"I hate to say that you are fortunate for what you have suffered, Colonel, but I believe you are and that at least some of your wounds will largely heal."

"Some?"

"We covered your eyes because the left one looks to have been permanently destroyed by a piece of shrapnel."

"Blind?" It was something Fitzwilliam could not grasp. "And the right?"

"We did not believe it to have been hit or affected but we wanted to cover it."

The surgeon's voice trailed away. The shock of what the colonel was hearing and feeling had a strangely calming effect on him.

"Major, can you get me a candle?" the surgeon asked.

He gave a slight squeeze of the patient's hand. "And now we will see—"

"If I can see."

"Yes, Colonel. We will see if you can see."

The doctor lifted the patient's head slightly and pulled the blindfold up. He then delicately completed its removal from the face. Its front was covered in blood, but only in one part. That part, which had been over the left eye, was soaked to a dark crimson, plain even in the low light. It was a delicate operation to strip the material from where it had become attached to the flesh. The eye itself was surrounded by puss. It was plainly gone.

The right one, on the other hand, seemed untouched. After blinking it several times, the colonel could vaguely *see* the surgeon holding the candle up with Major Groeper standing beside him. Mr. Reynolds moved the candle and lightly touched the skin around the socket.

The colonel saw that he was not in fact in the tent whence the worst of the screaming was coming and the limbs were being amputated and more than a few lives were draining away with each passing minute. Instead, he was out in the open and as far as he could tell he was in one of row upon row of cots as the doctors and nurses and aides considered who was to go where and when.

His observations were interrupted by the surgeon's softened voice. "I am very pleased, sir. It seems to have made it through."

"Thank God," the colonel repeated. "What of the rest of me?"

"It is mostly your left leg. I will leave it to the major to tell you what happened but for now I must go to others."

The colonel could see that the surgeon's apron too was drenched with blood and the sounds of the screaming men again washed over him.

"But." The surgeon stood. "I believe your leg wounds will largely heal. You may always have a limp, but I think that is all and before you ask, I will tell you that in my view you will be able to ride as all cavalrymen must be able to do."

He gave the colonel an reassuring pat on the arm.

In the low light of the candle and with his one eye, the colonel could see a slight smile from the exhausted man who nodded, handed the candle to Major Groeper, and was on to more desperate men.

The major took the surgeon's place on the small, wooden chair. He was still in the uniform he had worn in the battle, and it was caked in mud with a fair amount of blood as the colonel noticed with his one good eye. He, however, did not appear to have himself been injured, a fact the younger man seemed embarrassed to admit when asked.

"I do not know what you remember, sir. Nothing could stop the men. They went on, took a great many of the enemy's guns, and then, instead of halting, charged the lancers and cuirassiers. At this moment, I lost sight of the general, who was killed, and we cut my way to the rear, we being completely overpowered. We were nearing our lines with the French chasing us. The infantry had formed a box, and we were about to go through when a bit of French artillery exploded nearby."

He shook his head recalling the scene.

"I was next to you, and you and your horse went down. As did three or four others. The rest of us dismounted and grabbed you and the others, excepting one who was dead—Corporal Owens I think it was—and dragged you into one of the boxes.

"When the French attack was finally beaten back and the infantry advanced, we pulled you to some wagons and got you to the surgery and that's where you've been ever since."

"And the battle, Major? What of the battle?"

"It was very difficult. Those of us who could, returned to the fight and so many fell with each attack. Only when we had the field could I discover your fate, and I have been here ever since."

"But you say we won?"

"Aye, sir. The regiment had really beaten the French but some of the men were too excited and kept charging, and before we could control them, the French were on them."

"Did we lose many?"

"It was awful."

"Yes, that I do remember. And finally getting some order and beginning our retreat."

"Chaos, sir, that's what it was. Chaos. But we nearly made it."

"Who did not make it?"

"Well, the general, of course. I do not know if you saw that. I did not. But I'm told he was surrounded by French lancers and before he could surrender some of the Scots Greys tried to save him and they and the general were all butchered, sir. That's at least what I've been told."

"The Duke?"

"Oh, he's well, sir, though he was everywhere during the battle. We hear that Providence spared him without so much as a splinter even with that grand nose of his. That word spread quickly, including here, when we heard that Bonaparte had fled and that the Imperial Guard was decimated. Scores of cannon were captured and who knows how many Frenchmen."

This was quite enough for the moment. "Thank you, Major. I think I must rest."

"I'm right here, sir."

"No, Major. Go and get something to eat. You are no good to anyone if you are hungry. Get yourself cleaned up and come back. I am not going anywhere."

The major could not hide his own slight smile. "I can see that, sir," and he was gone.

The colonel was left to struggle with his great pain, diverting himself by thinking on what he had been told.

It was a great victory. It was a great cost, and many suffered far worse than he had. But it was a victory that perhaps meant after all these years, decades really, there could be peace and he could go back to being just another gentleman officer whose father could afford to purchase a commission for him.

When the major returned, he told the colonel that he would soon be moved to a more accommodating place, which was being set up some distance from the battlefield itself.

"You must do something for me, Major."

"Anything, sir. Frankly I would quite like to have something to do beyond taking parties out to collect the dead and dying."

"I ask that you write to several people. I'm sure an official dispatch will be sent to my father."

"The earl?"

"Indeed. But I want certain of my relations to hear that, however imperfectly, I have survived. Can you do that?"

"Of course."

The major reached into his tunic and pulled out a sheet of paper, a foreshortened quill pen, and a bottle of ink.

"It will be a simple message. That I have been wounded but am expected to largely recover from my injuries. Nothing beyond that. Make sure to use that word, *largely*. I do not want to deceive them if I can avoid it. I leave it to you to say it the way it needs to be said."

"And to whom?"

"I think to my brother Lord Ashworth in London and to my aunt and cousin, Lady Catherine de Bourgh and Anne, who are in Rosings Park in Kent. And, most importantly, to my other cousin Fitzwilliam Darcy. And you may assure him that he may assure his wife. He should be in London, on Brook Street now. You may be more graphic with him, but not too graphic. I spoke about him to you before the battle. I leave it to you."

11.

The sun was high and the air very, very warm and sticky when the colonel again awoke later on the morning after the battle. He had dozed off and when he woke up, the major was back in his chair, in which he had fallen asleep. He was startled awake by the colonel's movement.

When the major asked the colonel his condition, the colonel said that being alive must be deemed a victory of sorts.

"I may wish they had cut my leg off, though," he said before explaining the insistent, throbbing pain there. There was not anything to be said to that, so the major remained silent.

And now, although the greatest fear, of lying rotting on the battlefield, had not been realized, he was not out of danger. Encouragingly, though, with each passing hour, it seemed less likely that it would *come to that*. The throbbing pain in the colonel's head and leg and the unremitting screaming all about him nearly drove him to insanity. But he survived the day and he was glad he was far enough from the battlefield not to hear the horrors he knew were washing across from the dying men and horses, hoping that his own favorite mount had not suffered long.

When Mr. Reynolds came by early on the Tuesday, he dared quip that the fact that the colonel had survived the night was in his favour, the alternative apparently not being such a promising omen. What's more, the surgeon judged him sufficiently stable so as to be among the initial group of senior officers who would be sent to the coast and across to Dover and home to recuperate.

"It will be getting warm and the air will become more fetid, and I would like to begin to move you now. I am still concerned about infection, I believe, but you will have a better chance if we get you started home."

He waved to some orderlies who were assisting in the camp, and they carefully placed the colonel on a stretcher. This they carried between rows and rows of men, many having lost their voices for screaming and reduced to pitiful moaning and many more having lost their arms and legs with scarlet-soaked cloths wrapped around what remained of their limbs.

The colonel could only stare at the blue above him, aware that Major Groeper was walking behind the men bearing him. He did not know whether he deserved to be treated in this way, that he deserved to be sent from the field and home so early, but it was the way of his world. While God may not care that he was a senior officer, his fellow soldiers did and bore no grudge.

After being carried for nearly twenty minutes he calculated, they reached an open area. A series of wagons was lined up side-by-side, each sunk slightly into the sodden ground. Each had been fitted so that stretchers could be placed across lengthwise, and four could be loaded on each wagon. Each had an old field-horse in the harness.

The soldiers slowly and deliberately lifted the colonel's stretcher and moved it so it was right behind the driver's bench. They latched it down with ropes on either end. Even before they were finished, a second stretcher was placed on the wagon next to the colonel's. This process continued for two more officers.

None of them dared look to see who the others were and said no more than pass on their rank and their regiment. The colonel recognised none of them. He and the others remained alone in their thoughts. The colonel was somewhat drowsy from the movement of being carried. He closed his eyes, hoping without success to blot out the sounds and the smells of chaos and disorder all around him and through his dry lips he resumed the prayer he had begun shortly before the regiment headed into the muddy field for its first charge, a prayer he had returned to again and again since.

The major had said something about accompanying the colonel home, but it did not register and as the wagon began its movement along the potted trail, the rocking and the relief about moving lulled him to sleep. His wagon was one in a caravan of nearly a score of them, each with four seriously injured officers who had the expectation, or at least the hope, that they would survive their injuries and the trip itself.

Wellington had dispatched a battalion of cavalry that was held in reserve and not used at any of the battles in the recent days. It provided security for the injured, no one knowing whether there might be remnants of Bonaparte's defeated army roaming the countryside looking for easy prey and revenge.

The roads were still wet from the recent rain and things went very slowly. With each stop, the wagons were surveyed, and once or twice what had become an officer's lifeless body was moved to the wagon at the rear of the train and adjustments made with those still living. One of the officers, a major in the Foot Guards, originally on the wagon with the colonel, died on the Thursday. By then, the men were conscious enough to be able to speak for brief periods and began to turn into a curious band of brothers.

12.

Not long after the colonel and the others began their slow journey to the north and home and, they hoped and prayed, recovery, official word of Wellington's victory reached London. The joy was even greater than it had been the prior year because this time it was universally agreed that Bonaparte would be sent to a place far, far away and that he would never, ever have the opportunity to again return to his beloved France and he would never be able to raise an army to challenge the peace that the allies had finally and bloodily established.

The next day, Darcy attempted to go to the War Office to see what information he could gather with regard to the two men he knew who had been in the fighting, his cousin Colonel Fitzwilliam and his wife's brother-in-law Captain Wickham. When his cab neared the majestic building, the cabbie slowed as a jam of carriages failed to move.

"What is it, man?" asked Darcy through the window.

"I do not know, sir, but it looks like there's no getting through at least for now."

Suddenly fuming, Darcy shoved open the door. On the street, he handed his fare to the cabbie, seeing for himself how clustered the other carriages were in front of him. He began to walk the block or two to the War Office, but the pavement, too, was chock-a-block with unmoving men. They were all likely on the same mission as was Darcy.

When he got close enough to the front of the building, he heard an officer call out that they did not have any information about any regiment or soldier. Not a word.

"It's unprecedented," he called several times, each one in a different direction. "Come back tomorrow and we may have something. We have nothing now, so please go home."

Darcy was perturbed with himself for not realizing that this was the likely outcome of his trip. That it was too soon for anything of substance to have made its way to town.

The scene with its unmoving mob of all variety of London life, not merely London society, was repeated on the next day. The day after that was Sunday, so there would be nothing said at the War Office even if there was something to be said, which Darcy doubted there would be.

On Monday morning, though, as Darcy was finishing his breakfast and preparing to resume his quest for information, there was a ring at the door and a moment later, his cousin Lord Ashworth was announced.

"Cousin?" Darcy asked as he stood.

"Oh, sit down, Darcy. Sit down."

When his instruction was complied with, the visitor said he had received a letter not half an hour earlier from the War Office.

"It said my brother is injured but is *expected* to recover. No more. No less. That is what it said. It was so damn, pardon my expression, vague, Darcy. So damn vague."

He stepped to the sideboard on which cups and saucers and utensils were set out and after taking one of the cups and one of the saucers, he poured coffee from a pot into the former. He lifted the cup and took a drink of it, his face contorting at the bitterness, giving a slight shake before he restored his cup to the saucer and restored the both of them to the sideboard.

He began to walk, now looking out the window to the front, now looking at the large landscape above the sideboard.

"It is so vague, cousin."

"I'm sure they can only know so much of his condition."

His lordship stopped his pacing.

"That is it. I know it. But it remains so damn vague. Do you not agree? What's to be done about it?"

Darcy stood and got nearer his cousin.

"We must be patient. There are thousands of dead or injured, I imagine, my lord. They cannot send messengers to the families of each of them. They cannot know the true condition of any of them, including your brother. We must wait."

Darcy would not admit to the churning in his stomach about hearing the news. *It could have been worse* was the best he could think about it. *It could be worse.*

Lord Ashworth was promptly off to his nearby house, and Darcy climbed to the second floor. He rapped lightly on Elizabeth's door and received a "come in" in return.

His wife was in a dressing gown, sitting at her small desk writing with a cup of tea beside her sheet of stationery.

"What is it, my dear?" She was startled by the interruption and the look on Darcy's face. "Is it the war?"

He sat on the side of her bed and her heart fell.

"Yes. It is Richard. He is alive and expected to recover but the War Office has told his brother that he has been injured. There is nothing further that they apparently know about it. Just that he is injured but is expected to recover."

Elizabeth got off of her bench and went to him, sitting beside him on the bed. She grasped his hand and squeezed it, repeating that he was expected to recover.

Darcy could only nod, a slight tear forming in his eye, which he extinguished with a quick motion by his free hand.

He is expected to recover.

With a sigh, he rose. He suggested they go for an early walk when she was prepared, it being a bright but not warm London morning. And so they walked amid the cluster of pedestrians on the pavement, largely silent to and leaning lightly against one another, he with his thoughts, she with hers.

When they returned, a well-worn letter was sitting on a tray on the table in the foyer.

"I do not recognize the handwriting," he said to Elizabeth as he examined it. Without further ado, still standing by the table, he opened it. It was Major Groeper's initial letter, with the colonel himself, through his Major, telling his cousin that he was in fact injured but was expected to largely make a recovery. That this came from the colonel himself was an incredible relief, even given its want of real information, and the Darcys hugged each other quite inappropriately in the eyes of several members of staff but they did not care a whit for that. Not a whit.

They would learn his true condition soon enough. For that moment, though, it was enough that he was alive and was expected to recover. Both remained silent about the particular adverb used. "Largely." But they both needed it

In light of what he saw when he tried to get information from the War Office and the scant information that Lord Ashworth had from that bureaucracy, Darcy decided to wait several days to venture back to inquire about Wickham. On the Thursday, he received a more detailed letter that Groeper had written for the colonel. It came with the morning mail, and he discovered it when he returned from a ride with Bingley in Hyde Park.

"Has Mrs. Darcy seen this?" he asked Jones, the butler, and was told that she had, having returned from her regular walk with Jane and Georgiana not half an hour before. "She lifted it and saw who it was addressed to, Sir, and returned it."

It was, in fact, far thicker than the prior one from Groeper. Darcy decided to read it first and immediately before showing it to his wife.

Realizing its length, and *fearing* its length, he went alone into his study on the first floor. He poured himself a whisky from one of the crystal decanters kept on a small bar. With the letter vibrating slightly in his left hand and his whisky in his more stable right, he lowered himself into his favorite chair. He began to read. It was what he was waiting for, and its contents confirmed some of his greatest fears and lifted some of his strongest hopes:

Somewhere in the Netherlands

Thursday, June 22, 1815

Fitzwilliam Darcy
Brook Street
London

Mr. Darcy.

Sir. As you know from my recent short note, I am Major Michael Groeper, an aide to your cousin, Colonel Richard Fitzwilliam. He has requested that I write to you to advise you of his current condition.

Rest assured that we believe the worst of it is over and that he is no longer in grave danger. He is far from well, but the doctors have expressed the view that he will largely recover. We are at this moment among a convoy of wagons removing injured officers toward the Channel so that they can be transported back to England.

This group is among those capable of being transported. The conditions near the battlefield are very dire and sadly death is far more common than you can imagine. That the colonel is among this group being transported is a sign of the confidence of the doctors.

The colonel is at times in great pain. To be blunt, he has suffered the loss of his left eye and his left leg has suffered a grievous injury but he is fortunate that he was not forced to have it amputated as so many others did. Many who suffered the amputation have died soon thereafter.

Darcy placed the letter down on his lap, looking into the distance. *So it is quite bad. Not fatal. But he will never be the same.* There was more, but the major—in the most efficient manner of an officer in the King's Army—had been simple and direct. An eye lost. A permanent limp.

He closed his eyes and inhaled, ready to continue. But not before putting the letter in his left hand, lifting the glass from the small table to his right on which he had placed it. He savored the smooth liquor as he tasted and swallowed it and returned the glass and what was left of the whisky to the table. He again held the letter up in both his hands.

I am among the group riding alongside the wagons, providing some level of protection, though at this point we have not been disturbed by any enemy forces. We are hopeful that with the battle won, Bonaparte will have been taken care of. Of course, I am not privy to official dispatches concerning that, but the lack of any effort to interfere with our progress suggests it is true.

The colonel sleeps much of the time but he and I have been able to converse, particularly when we stop for rest and a change of horses. We have been told to expect that he will be transferred to a carriage when we are in the vicinity of Ghent, which should drastically improve his condition.

I turn now to other news.

Darcy again lifted his glass. He took a final amount of the whisky. For a moment he considered getting more but he thought better of it, it not having yet reached midday. After the glass was again on the table, he resumed his reading with a deep breath, to get to this other news.

You will have heard many reports of varying accuracy concerning the recent battle. I will limit myself to your cousin's involvement in it. I hope that it assists your understanding of events.

The weather was frightful the night before. It rained and rained, which was an ill omen for we cavalrymen. But it proved ill to Bonaparte as well. He seems to have delayed commencing his maneuvers until the ground hardened somewhat. His delay allowed allied troops to appear— especially the Prussians—while the battle was still hot.

Our own Regiment, the First Royal Dragoons, found the ground very soft and our "charge" was hardly a charge at all. It did, however, prove a success at first. The colonel led the way, sword waving high, as we encountered and destroyed a large group of French infantry.

Alas, for no fault of the colonel or other officers, the men were too raw, and they and their horses could not be held back after the smell of blood had gotten into them and they kept riding. They rode too far, and we were set upon by French lancers. Our great general, General Sir William Ponsonby, found himself in difficulty and as a group of the Scots Greys from our regiment sought to rescue him, they and he were cut down.

The colonel somehow managed to get some control over our troops, and he led us back towards our line so we could regroup and return once more into the fray. Alas, just as he was nearly there, a shell from French artillery to our right flank exploded near him. The wet ground prevented the ball from bouncing, but in this case the ground was hard enough for it to burst apart and send shrapnel every which way.

Sadly, some of that found the colonel as well as his horse Atlas. He was thrown down and another officer and I were able to dismount and drag him into an opening made for us in one of our squares.

There he remained for some time in the blood and mud as those of us who were able to continue the fight found horses for several further charges into the French until the infantry began the final assault on the French troops, including, I have been told, the Imperial Guard! A French Eagle was also captured.

By God's will, I was unharmed. I accompanied the colonel as he was evacuated to a field to the rear. It was a horrible scene that I fear will never leave me but imagine a ring of hell and you will have some slight notion of the conditions. I will not speak more of it. I cannot, sir, speak more of it.

*   *   *   *

I have dictated this letter to your cousin as he is unable to write himself. He endorses what I have said although he insists that I give him more credit for his conduct on the battlefield than he deserves. I assure you that this is not the case.

I do not know when you will receive this. I will continue to write to you to advise you of his condition and of our journey, which I believe will ultimately be to your house in London.

I pray that with each letter we will be nearer to reaching you and the colonel will be nearer to recovering as well as any man can recover after what he has been through.

Finally, the colonel has asked that you not share this letter with anyone except your dear wife, for whom he has the greatest admiration. You are free to tell others in general *terms the news this letter conveys but he believes, and I agree, that the intimacy of this communication need not be shared.*

I am, &c., &c.
Michael Groeper
Major,
First Royal Dragoons

Darcy folded the letter and restored it to its envelope. He stood, placing the package on the side table and taking up his whisky. *No, too much, too early*, he thought as he merely cradled the glass, recalling that it was empty, as he gazed out onto Brook Street. *What shall I tell the others? Elizabeth.* He looked down at the glass. *I cannot help but tell my sister. I know he would have allowed it had he had the notion that she would be sharing our roof with us when I received it. I must tell Georgiana, too.*

He restored his glass to the sideboard and took up the envelope. He now understood the major's use of "largely expected to recover" in his short initial dispatch. He would never recover that eye. He would always have a limp. But he was alive and interesting as the details of the battle as recited by the major were on first reading, they paled in comparison to the reality that he was alive, and he was coming home to them. Battered but not beaten.

He expected that Elizabeth would be in her study. Normally, she had be removing her walking clothes and beginning to change into something more casual for the rest of the day, no visitors being expected and no visits to be made. He knew her too well, though, to think she would do what she ordinarily did having seen the envelope in the foyer.

He was right. He knocked on her study door, and she herself opened it.

"You have read it, I see," she said as he came in, nodding to the object dangling from his fingers. He held it to her. "Is it bad?" she asked.

She took it. "I can only say it could be far, far worse but I believe our Richard will be returning to us, injured but alive."

She nodded again as she opened the envelope. She sat in one of a pair of comfortable armchairs that stood either side of an oval table in one corner. She extracted the letter itself and placed the envelope on that small table. Darcy stood, observing her and especially her face as he imagined where she was in the major's words. He was glad that the major had been direct and had placed the most important part early on, and he knew his wife had reached that point when she thrust the letter down into her lap when he understood that she read of his disfigurement much as he had done.

"Oh, Fitzwilliam. It is so awful."

He lowered himself to the other chair, and just in time to run a finger across her cheek to intercept a tear that was slowly streaming down.

"My dear. I know he will come through this. I know he will. And he will need us to do so."

She nodded. "The balance of the letter" he said, "is talk of the events of the battle. I do not know if you should read it now. It is of more historical interest than anything. It speaks of his and his colleagues' bravery and…and the horrors of it all."

He extended his hand, and she returned the letter to him, placing it in the envelope he collected from the table.

"He expressly authorizes me to speak to you of the contents but that I am not to tell anyone else anything more than the most general information. They are to be told that he has been seriously injured but is expected to recover even if he will bear permanent scars."

Elizabeth nodded.

"But I think I must share it with Georgiana."

Elizabeth was not sure.

"I think he would have allowed it, she being the only other member of my family, had he known that she was with us. She is well old enough to understand. I do think she would feel betrayed if I or my cousin were not completely honest with her. She will discover it soon enough."

Elizabeth rose and went to the window that looked out to the house's rear. Darcy remained in his chair, watching her stiffen before she turned back.

"I agree. I believe, dearest, that it must be you who speaks to her. I do not believe that having her read the letter would be appropriate, but telling the particulars of his injuries is something you must do. We can be as vague as we would like as to the others. But we three are deeply among his family and I think it must be done."

13.

Darcy had seen his sister collapse in agony in a maelstrom of emotion and disappointment once before. It was when she was fifteen and he had intercepted a scheme by George Wickham and Mrs. Younge to take her to Gretna Green and make her his wife. And to make her fortune his.

Now she was a different creature. A woman and not a girl. After discussing the letter Groeper had written with the colonel's blessing, Darcy and Elizabeth had found Georgiana sitting in the house's fine library, in one of the comfortable chairs that Elizabeth had imported to enhance the room's purpose as a place to sit and read. In this case, Georgiana had been sitting with a novel written by *A Lady* near a window that opened to the rear of the house. She had looked up when she heard a rapping on the door and then the appearance of her brother. Elizabeth had waited in the hallway, unobserved, the door slightly ajar.

"Is it our cousin?" she had asked as she closed her book before her brother was two steps into the room.

He had nodded and she had then hurried to him, hugging him much as his wife had so recently done. Then she pushed away from him and looked up at his face.

"Is he dead?"

"No, Georgie. He is not dead." He had patted her on the back as he had often done. "He is not dead. He wrote through his aide, a major, with details of his cousin's condition. Richard is hurt and has...has lost the sight in his left eye and has a limp but should otherwise survive his wounds. He is already being transported home and we hope he will be here soon."

She looked at him. He nodded. It was as if a shot rang through her. The shock of the news from the colonel proved too much and Darcy was just in time to catch her before she fell to the ground. He was able to remove her to a sofa there while he rang so that smelling salts could be administered to her.

Elizabeth, who had been pacing outside the room, rushed in right behind the footman who was responding to Darcy's call. She went to the sofa and knelt as Darcy's instructions were being complied with. She rubbed her hands across her sister's cheeks and murmured "sweet Georgiana" to her several times.

The footman soon returned with the salts, and Elizabeth opened the bottle and ran in below Georgiana's nose, which led the young woman to shoot awake with a shutter. Elizabeth closed the bottle and handed it back to the footman.

"No one is to know about this. Is that understood?"

"Yes, ma'am," he said in terror as he took the bottle and promptly vacated the room.

When Georgiana had begun to recover, Darcy said, "This is all we know but we must think it good news."

"In light of the alternative?" she mumbled.

"I'm afraid that that is the case, yes."

Darcy was left helpless, having no idea what to do as Elizabeth took charge. He made himself inconspicuous by the room's windows, looking out but listening carefully to whatever was happening behind him.

When he heard Georgiana apologizing for being such a silly girl, he turned, to discover that his sister had rotated herself so as to be sitting on the sofa and that Elizabeth was beside her with her arm around her and whispering something in her ear that Darcy could not make out but to which Georgiana nodded. He strode to the sofa and squatted down.

"Are you recovered, my dear? Do you recall what I said to you?"

She nodded, running her dress's sleeve beneath her nose in an attempt to restore some element of decency after her tantrum. He gave her his handkerchief, which she quickly put to good use to remove her tears. She caught her breath.

"Oh, brother. Tell me he will still be Richard."

Darcy looked at Elizabeth who nodded.

"He may have been marred, but he must always be Richard, and we must always remember that." It was her turn to nod.

Darcy sat in an armchair that was at an angle to the sofa.

"I did not have the opportunity to tell you that he does not wish *anyone* other than us"—he was being delicate on her inclusion—"to know the details of what has happened. You must say nothing about it. He will be here soon enough, God willing, and we must leave it to him and his Major friend to address that issue. He wished us to know the magnitude of his injuries and no one else, and we must respect that."

She nodded again and said "I understand but I do not know who in the world I might tell." She smiled as she gripped Elizabeth's hand with one of her own and leant forward to take one of her brothers with the other.

From that point, shorter letters were received on Brook Street almost every other day by (or for) the colonel and the others being transported after the initial chaos in the battle's aftermath. The Army had made accommodations for the fast transport of such senior officers' letters, and as for those about the colonel they told of improvements in his condition.

14.

The optimism concerning the colonel's condition and prospects increased with each succeeding letter from Major Groeper. The colonel's spirits were lifting with his realization of the victory and his gradual acceptance of his limits. The pain, too, was gradually diminishing, though there were still moments when he again thought of how it would have been a blessing to have had his left leg simply lopped off.

The major was always there for him. The seas were calm but there was a good easterly wind, and the wounded were placed on the transport ship's deck with the aides nearby for the crossing to Dover.

Once back on English soil, the injured were in carriages heading north and were lauded at each city and town and village and even crossroad they passed *en route*.

The cavalrymen such as Major Groeper who had accompanied them across the Low Countries were no longer afraid of an ambush. They now generally rode ahead or behind the caravan and as it neared a town, one or two front riders rushed ahead to announce their approach.

More than one mayor offered to have a ball held in their honor, but the primary aim of everyone on the move was to get to London, where they would all finally be able to rest and consider what was to happen to them.

* * * *

Much news of the battle preceded the caravan's arrival in London. And as Major Groeper predicted, much of it was wrong for there had been no English reporters anywhere near the battlefield. Within the week, though, an accurate sense of the victory had been established. As *The Observer* wrote one week after the battle:

> *Every incident relating to the late battle is so interesting and honorable to the national character, and the source of so much commendable pride and exultation to every Englishman, and at the same time so much sought after, that we have been induced to collect them from every conceivable source and present them to our readers. But we cannot refer to these without expressing gratification that our pages are emblazoned with fresh proud records of British velour. Heaven has, indeed, smiled on the good cause of freedom and of loyalty, and victory has twined her brightest wreath to decorate the brows of Wellington.*
>
> *Dreadful has been the struggle, and awful indeed, the sacrifice, and even the splendid results of the 18th June have been dearly purchased at the expense of the rich blood shed on the memorable occasion; but in the successful issue of this arduous contest, we may confidently anticipate the speedy destruction of the cause of all the evils which have desolated the Continent for so many years, and the restoration of peace to Europe and the Universe, whose beams have been so sweet and transient.*

Darcy read this report in his library after having attended Sunday services. At the services, the battle was spoken of and the men who had served were the subject of the congregation's prayers. By then, he, Elizabeth, and the others in his household and in the Bingleys' knew too well that some of the blood came from his dear cousin.

15.

Even as he was receiving letters from Major Groeper during the colonel's return to England, Darcy took it upon himself to visit the War Office every few days to see if there was any news about George Wickham's regiment and particularly about George Wickham himself. It was how he received word that although a tally had been received of the dead and wounded in that regiment, Captain Wickham's name was not on it. He immediately had a dispatch sent to Longbourn with this news, albeit with the caveat that he had not received confirmation that Wickham was in fact unharmed. He included a promise to his sister-in-law that he would send further intelligence he received about the Captain the moment it reached him.

Several days after that, he was told that not only was Captain Wickham uninjured, thank the Lord, but he was mentioned favorably in the commanding officer's dispatch about the battle and that he was in line for some sort of commendation for the way he conducted himself in the heat of battle. This news was promptly transmitted to Mrs. Wickham with the further explanation that it was expected that seeing that there was little left to be done by most of the men in Wellington's army, the process of returning home would begin in less than a fortnight's time. Wickham's regiment would, Darcy was told and passed on to Lydia, be returning to its headquarters outside of Newcastle.

In the flush of excitement, Lydia began the process of making herself ready to be there when her husband returned in triumph. Then Darcy received a message from the War Office saying that there had been a change of plans. Wickham's regiment was selected among those to parade in London itself and would be encamped near Chelsea until it would return to Newcastle after the festivities.

The wonder of it, his wife understood. She was soon to be reunited with her hero. Now she and Catherine and her parents could not delay in going up to town, much as her parents did not like to venture there.

16.

Neither the colonel nor the major could or wished to give full breath to the slow progress home. And then they were back. Though the colonel considered imposing on his brother for his recuperation in London, Lord Ashworth had a wife and three young children and was committed to numerous outside activities. Thus the colonel gladly accepted his cousin's invitation to stay on Brook Street for as long as he wished.

*　*　*　*

Although the Darcy house was festooned with celebratory bunting as were its neighbors, the family kept matters as sedate as possible until the colonel had settled in, and his wishes could be taken account of. The carriage with him and the major arrived early on a Thursday afternoon and as several footmen took care of bringing the trunks into the house and to the bedchambers designated for the guests, Elizabeth and Darcy and Georgiana greeted them on the pavement.

To the Darcys, the actual *seeing* the colonel was a major relief. Their worst fears were not realized. He had a patch over his left eye and there were several short scars on his left cheek. He was otherwise quite well attired in his albeit well-worn uniform.

Rooms for the two were on the second floor. Darcy had wondered whether it was best to assign a room on the ground floor to him, but Elizabeth insisted that it was preferable that he be close to the family.

Coffee and some cakes were laid out. The colonel selected what had long been a favorite chair. It was not too far from the window and offered a fine view out to the street.

"We hope you will find your accommodations to your satisfaction," Darcy said.

The colonel laughed. "Oh, Darcy, you can have no idea about the level of accommodations the major and I have endured these past months. A tent on dry ground would be a veritable palace for us."

"Well," Elizabeth interrupted, "we hope that we can do at least slightly better than that. And we, honestly, hope that you will have no difficulties in reaching them."

"Mrs. Darcy, again, do not think me a piece of porcelain. Your stairs will be nothing to me, with the major's help, and will be the means for quickening my recovery."

He looked from Elizabeth to Darcy. "Now, please, you must treat me as a visiting relative. No more. No less."

Georgiana joined them, and the five became comfortable, chatting about nothings.

"There were times, many times, when I doubted I could ever again enjoy the simple pleasures of looking out onto a London street and the people passing anonymously by."

The others let him gaze out, and after a minute or so he turned back into the room.

"Now, let's talk about what is to happen to me and to the major."

Darcy took up the conversation.

"I have spoken to your brother, and I think he quite understands the situation. When we are done here, I will send him a note giving him my assessment of your condition now that I have seen you."

"And what is your assessment?"

"Frankly, that you seem to be in far better condition, with one notable exception, than we had reason to expect. Stories of the injuries suffered have been flooding into town and they can be intolerable to hear, let alone the stories of those who succumbed. But having now seen you and having spoken to you, I think I may tell your brother that you seem to have suffered greatly but are not so badly damaged—again with that one notable exception—that we need despair of you largely recovering."

"Fitzwilliam, the reality is that I have lost one of my eyes. I am learning to live with just the right one. I have a limp. I will always have a limp but with each day I am more confident that I will be able to ride, as the surgeon told me I would. I am very fortunate, and I know that. If there is one thing people must understand it is that I am still who I was when I left England. A little beaten down. But still much the same."

He looked over at Elizabeth.

"Mrs. Darcy, for God's sake, I will not tolerate tears from you or from anyone else." He looked at his cousin Georgiana. "Nor from you."

"I'm just…I'm just so relieved is all," Georgiana said in fits and starts. "We were so worried when my brother reported what he had been told by the War Office, and we got that first note."

"Did it not say I would be alright?"

"But you are a soldier. You and the major, both," Elizabeth said as she nodded to the latter gentleman, who sat somewhat embarrassed to the colonel's right, "and you have to say things like that even if they are not true. So I'm afraid we did not fully believe you, even in the letters the major wrote to us on your behalf."

"Oh, my dear Mrs. Darcy, now you must believe what you see. Now and, I hope, in the days to come."

"If I may continue," Darcy interrupted. "Your brother is of course most anxious to see you. I met with him not two days ago. He does not wish, as he put it, to *overexcite you* and will do what he can to appear before you the moment you wish it."

"I suggest then, Darcy, that you have him and his wife visit us tomorrow afternoon."

And so it was arranged and as he was tired, the colonel asked that he be excused to lie down before dinner. The major helped him to his room and left him only when the colonel insisted that he do so.

*   *   *   *

It was likely past midnight when Elizabeth was roused by a sound. The window of her bedchamber was open and beyond the curtain a bit of summer rain could be heard, lightly hitting. This sound, though, was from the other direction, outside her door. While it would normally not be of interest to her, on this night she was anxious with the presence of their guests. She lifted a light robe from a chair near her bed and guided herself with her hands through the dark room until she could see light below the door.

Upon reaching it, she listened. It was plain that the footman on duty through the night had passed by to go to the kitchen down the servants' stairs. Opening her door and looking out, she saw light at the end of the hallway, coming from the colonel's room. She ventured in that direction and, the door being open, she knocked very lightly on it.

The sound startled the officer. There was a single candle on a bedside table illuminating the room. He had been sitting in one of his own chairs near the window but rose awkwardly when he heard her.

"Mrs. Darcy! I pray I did not disturb you. I was having some difficulty sleeping and I asked for some ale to help relax me."

"Oh, Colonel, you are our guest, and you could not possibly disturb me even in the nighttime. May I come join you?"

She could make out his nod and he pointed to the twin of his own chair, which she took.

Their brief silence was ended by the colonel, speaking softly in the night air.

"I did not have the chance to tell you when I came for the wedding but I was not entirely surprised when I received Darcy's note about you and he marrying."

These first words surprised Elizabeth.

He continued. "You will recall, I hope, our pleasant stroll at Rosings."

"Of course. It was most delightful—"

"Yet it ended with us both being too aware of the limitations we each faced as to marriage."

She smiled at the memory. "Indeed it did. It was, I think, our discussion of the reality of the world."

"The very word I used with Darcy afterwards."

"Afterwards?"

"You see—" He adjusted himself in his chair so as to be able to lean more intimately towards her. "I suspected from the day I met you—"

"At the Parsonage?"

"I admit that even then I suspected that he had some attractions towards you. It was the only explanation for his insistence that we accompany Mr. Collins back to the Parsonage when the vicar hurried to visit us—I mean Darcy, since he knew nothing of my presence—at the great house the morning after our arrival. The very morning. I questioned him about it on the way back to Lady Catherine's and he could not but admit that you were the cause. I, of course, did not know you beyond the pleasant time we had just spent that afternoon."

"Indeed, as I recall, my conversation with *you* was most pleasant though that with Mr. Darcy—"

"Was not. Yes, it is the very thing I told him, Mrs. Darcy."

"Of for goodness sakes, Richard, you must call me Lizzy."

"Then Lizzy it is."

"Good," she said. "Now that we have gotten that out of the way. But back to that conversation."

"I said that his taciturn nature can be quite discouraging to others and, as I say, it was a display of how different he and I are. And I so enjoyed our various later conversations, even the one we had when I came upon you alone in the Park."

"When you perhaps said more about your cousin than was prudent?"

"About your sister Jane? Yes. I only learned later the effect my attempt to improve your view of him was exactly the opposite of what I intended. Still," he said, leaning back in his chair but still keeping his voice low, "matters were resolved satisfactorily in the end."

"It was only later that he learned that what I said to him—"

"In rejecting his first offer—"

Lizzy was surprised. "So you know about that?" She had not known that *anyone* was privy to that little episode.

"*That* I learned when he felt compelled to justify our premature abandonment of our aunt's generosity."

"Yes," said Lizzy, "he may have been angry that I learned what he had done, or not done, with respect to Jane and Charles Bingley being in London at the same time."

They were quiet for a moment until she said, "In the end, though, it was of benefit to us both as he was forced by my anger about what was plain to me and I think ultimately became plain to him concerning his lack of true concern for his friend and for that friend's heart to consider his own actions."

The colonel—Richard—again leaned towards her to observe that, "A man like Fitzwilliam Darcy is not particularly adept at reconsidering his own actions."

"As I have learned. But I have discovered that he can be swayed to do so by a pleasant smile and fine pair of eyes."

Even in the low light he was reminded that she possessed a very fine pair of eyes indeed. "Things of which you just happen to possess."

"Indeed, Colonel Fitzwilliam. Or at least so my husband has told me."

"Knowing him quite well and knowing enough about *you* from our too brief meetings, from that moment of my conversation with him, I had every confidence if not expectation that should fate conspire to have you fall again into one another's company, his pride and your prejudice might be cast aside and, well, here we are."

"Yes, sir. Here we are." In the low light, he caught a glimmer of this intriguing woman's pleasant smile.

The footman arrived at this point, clearly surprised and flustered upon seeing his mistress sitting so nonchalantly with the colonel, but she set his mind at rest by rising to take the small tray from him and dismissing him.

The colonel took a long drink from the glass and felt the elixir flow down into him. She watched him closely as she resumed her seat.

When he put the crystal on the table that was between them, Elizabeth resumed.

"Now we must consider your own prospects."

"*My* prospects?"

"You will recall we spoke of them some time ago."

"On that fine stroll. Yes, I do recall. And I recall that we agreed that I required a small fortune, and you admitted that you required at least some fortune."

"Which you can see," and she spread her arms and offered a smile visible even in the flickering candlelight, "I have managed to obtain through guile and my womanly charms."

The colonel admitted to himself that he had never met a woman quite like this Elizabeth Darcy and wondered, not for the first time, what it would have been like to have wooed her before she was taken. No, he realized, this particular Bennet girl—he could not speak of the others—was the type who felt most at home with a man of depth and still waters, neither of which—he thought at least—applied to him.

"And now," she continued, "we must see just what you can obtain through your own guile and your not inconsiderable manly charms."

"Not as considerable as they once were."

"But formidable still, I daresay, and surely formidable enough for a woman of good sense, even if she lacks a great fortune."

"Is that not the rub? Has it not always been?"

She sat back while he reached for his glass to take another drink of his ale.

"Well, Richard, we shall have to see what can be done for you."

"We shall see." He took the final bit of ale from his glass and placed the crystal on the table. She began to stand, indicating that he should remain as he was.

"I hope you will be able to find sleep now and that it will not be unpleasant."

"Should I dream of you, Mrs. Darcy, I assure you that it will not be."

She blushed slightly and turned to go with a nod.

"Lizzy."

"Lizzy," said he.

With that she gave another nod and left, closing the door behind her. The footman was trying to remain awake on the chair close by the officer's room, and she nodded and smiled at him before continuing back to her own bedchamber. The rain was still coming and was perhaps even heavier than when she left. But she was well tired, and she found it soothed her and soon she heard it no more and fell into a deep sleep while, down the hall, the footman somehow managed to stay awake, and the colonel returned to the fine bed in his tasteful room and did not.

17

The colonel's brother and sister-in-law appeared at Brook Street in the early afternoon of the next day. Both of the brothers were surprised by the emotions brought to the surface when they were reunited. Lord Ashworth—the analytical one—asked again and again if there was anything—"*anything*"—he could do. And Lady Ashworth sat as near to her brother-in-law as she could and gripped his hand in her lap as she told him again and again how relieved they were that he had come through it.

Elizabeth and Lady Ashworth had been introduced to one another at a party held at Netherfield before Elizabeth's wedding. Now they sat close to each other, their cups replenished with a fine tea. Lady Ashworth seemed at first to be a quite plain woman in looks but it was not long before Elizabeth saw she was a sensible one, a Cambridge don's daughter after all, and they promised to visit with each other when they were both in town. Before the lord and lady left, Elizabeth also rang for the major to come and be properly introduced, which was pleasantly done.

At the colonel's request, though, visits from others were rationed.

* * * *

As for Georgiana Darcy, the major knew of her only from passing references by the colonel, made when he spoke of the various strands of his family. When he actually saw her, he was impressed. He thought her features much softer than were Darcy's. Her hair was a light brown almost tinged with auburn and a band of ringlets dangled across her forehead. For a fleeting moment he was tempted to reach and push the curls to the side were they to be at the point of such intimacy as to permit such a step.

While both Darcys were tall, she also differed from her brother in being very thin with arms that looked quite delicate. And though she appeared shy in the first meeting, he recognized that she was likely far more formidable than that first impression suggested. He immediately hoped he would have the opportunity to find out.

With those introductions out of the way, it was not long after the two officers' arrival that the household on Brook Street fell into the informality that was familiar to the three Bennet girls in town, that is Jane, Lizzy, and Mary.

The last of these had leave to play on Darcy's pianoforte when she visited and it was more tolerable and even enjoyable without the stridency she too often displayed at Longbourn and Meryton. She even played Mozart duets with Georgiana. For her part, Lizzy rarely took a turn on the keys.

It should be noted, though, that there was some nervousness by the discovery that Jane Bingley was in the family way! Her belly was noticeably round and several wondered whether Charles Bingley could possibly tolerate the anxiety until the blessed arrival of the child. This view being sobered by the universal fear that Jane would lose the child early.

Meanwhile, after a week or so, the colonel was going out more and more and for longer and longer. He often went just with the major, who was staying with his parents but who came to the Darcys' every morning and remained as often as not for dinner before returning to Cheapside. It was slow, but soon the pair of officers could reach Hyde Park, where they would find a bench and watch men parading on their horses, aware of which were military men and which had experience that at least at first went no further than riding to the hounds.

*   *   *   *

When word finally reached Darcy that Wickham's regiment would be arriving in Chelsea, he wrote to Longbourn with an invitation that the family come to town for the celebration and Mrs. Wickham's reunion with her husband. A response quickly came from Mr. Bennet. He thanked Darcy for the information and accepted the most gracious invitation.

"I do not wish to impose unduly, sir," he wrote, "and have requested the courtesy from my wife's brother for she and I to stay on Gracechurch Street. I will be much obliged to you if you and Mr. Bingley can find space for the keeping of my two remaining daughters."

Lizzy decided to separately write to Catherine since she would be living with the colonel back at Brook Street.

Brook Street

July 10, 1815

Dear Catherine,

Fitzwilliam and I are pleased that you will soon be returning to us. I write particularly with regard to Colonel Fitzwilliam. You will have heard of his injuries. Because you will be here with him and I have seen him, I want to assure you that although he has suffered serious injuries, most particularly the loss of an eye, he is well on the road to recovery.

War is a difficult matter, especially when it so affects someone you have great admiration and affection for, as I do with the colonel. I hope that you will come to have that as well. I write simply so you are prepared to see a man in his condition who remains in high spirits.

Lizzy

Appropriate arrangements were made. In the third week of the colonel's tenure at the Darcys and a week before Wickham and his regiment were to arrive in Chelsea, a carriage carrying the visitors from Hertfordshire reached town and deposited the various members of the Bennet family with their assigned hosts, where they were to be deposited, with a sufficient number of trunks to ensure that their stays would be comfortable.

When Catherine stepped from the coach, which had just deposited Lydia several blocks away at Jane's, she found the familiar trio of Lizzy, Darcy, and Georgiana. They exchanged courtesies and the women shared hugs.

They headed directly through the open door to the house's sitting room. Standing next to one another were the two officers as Elizabeth had whispered to Catherine that there would be. The reality as to the colonel was both harsher and easier than Catherine expected. Harsher in the seeing a man of such great physical stature plainly knocked down by the war. But somehow easier because the essence of the man did not seem much changed from when she saw him those months ago at Meryton.

Yes, he was plainly injured, most obviously with the patch across his eye. But he was in no way bowed by it and stood with the straightness one would expect of a British soldier.

And beside him was another fine specimen of the breed, introduced by Georgiana as the famous Major Groeper, the colonel's constant companion before, during, and, most tellingly, after the great battle. He was, even at first glance, a fine, young man.

The visitors all settled in quite readily. At the Bingleys' on Mount Street, Jane managed to keep Lydia tolerably content, by paying somewhat more attention than she normally would have and a great deal more attention than was deserved.

For her part, Mary was somewhat more civil to her youngest sister than she had been before. But not by much. She was content to cloister herself in her room with the religious tracts she collected from her church's bookstore.

As for her parents, the middle Bennet girl had scarce time for them and they had even less for her.

18.

Those at Longbourn arrived well before the grand parade. It was a joyous occasion for the country. The troopers marched past the Palace and up St. James's Park. They marched in the sort of order that the militia displayed in Meryton and that helped soften the hearts of all the women, young and old, who watched them. They were still soldiers that day though within a month many would be discharged.

The orderliness was not so convincing to many of the town's homes, including the Darcys' on Brook Street. These were homes where sons and husbands had not returned from the continent or where they returned but were not quite the same as they were when they marched away those months before.

The colonel attended the parade in his full dress uniform and sitting with members of his regiment and the others in the Union Brigade in a place of honor along the parade route, with the major and other survivors standing among them.

Afterwards, a dinner was held at the Bingleys'. The guest of honor was Captain George Wickham, and Lydia basked in his glow. In the house's grand drawing room, he mingled easily with the guests, often with his wife at his side. He properly gave his regards to the colonel, who stood as necessary but otherwise sat in a largely inconspicuous part of the room, next to the major and more often than not with both Catherine and Georgiana.

And Captain Wickham and several of his fellow officers who had come through the events at Waterloo made love to all the room excepting those other two officers and the Bennet sisters to whom he was not married. And at the soonest possible moment, after dinner was completed and while the sexes went to their various rooms before they would readjourn. The colonel and the major left for their rooms alone, insisting that Catherine and Georgiana remain as was their duty.

"He is such a grizzled old thing," Lydia said when she walked up to Catherine with the other ladies who had assembled in the drawing room. Both Georgiana and Lizzy had their eyes on the pair and their ears open. "It's a wonder that he showed his face to the far superior specimen that is my hero husband."

Catherine waited until Lydia completed this statement before simply saying that the colonel is a hero who is owed a debt by the nation and that in her view he is among the most pleasantly striking men of her acquaintance.

Lydia leaned in towards her sister, and her words were not heard by the others. Those words were, "You have always been jealous of what I have and what you will never have." She stepped back with a smile, which Catherine returned without a word and Lydia turned to find where her husband was and quickly went to him, triumphant in having put her annoying older sister in her place, though neither could know it, those were the last words expressed by one sister to the other. When Lydia left the Bingleys two days later to join her husband in the north, she did not notice that Catherine was not among those who came to see her off.

19.

Darcy took justifiable pride in the great library he and his father and his father's father had created at Pemberley. As a boy it was a great refuge for him and, at times, George Wickham, as they burrowed themselves into comfortable chairs and read adventure tales of the sort guaranteed to foster a boy's dreams of growing up and exploring the world. As a pirate.

On Brook Street, he had himself built a fine library in that tradition. It was not nearly so grand as the one in the country, but it was well organized and also had very comfortable spots for one to get lost in a story on a rainy autumn afternoon in Mayfair.

One of those who had come to enjoy its offerings was Colonel Fitzwilliam. He was not an avid reader in his family's own library at Haverford Hall but the boredom of army life with its hour upon hour of waiting and waiting had made something a reader out of him, as it had for many similarly thinly educated soldiers.

When he was settled at the Darcys' now in his damaged condition, it became his great refuge. The room was paneled in a fine rosewood. It had a single eight-over-eight window that looked to the rear of the house, a pair of light curtains on either side of it.

Armchairs and a matching sofa in a burgundy leather were centered in the room on an oriental carpet that was primarily blue with cream accents. There was some open space on the walls, on which fine horizontal landscapes of Derbyshire were hung. Two cloth chairs in matching patterned covers sat near the window. With a low, scalloped table in the wood that matched the paneling and shelving between them.

All paled in comparison to the room's prime attraction. Its books. The shelves did not rise to the height as did those at Pemberley but they were high enough to require the use of a set of three steps to reach the volumes on the uppermost shelves.

Within a day or two of his recent arrival, the colonel had rediscovered its charms. He had always found it a comfort on earlier visits, and so it was now, even in his altered state. He could be alone with his one good eye and a bit of his limp and his at times jumbled thoughts as he maneuvered from collection to collection, now and then pulling out a volume to peruse before restoring it. He saw the histories of Greece and Rome and England. He promised himself he would one day venture into them to advance himself as to such worldly things, but in his battered condition he first opted to select one of the four volumes from a favorite.

He had taken the first volume down. He flipped through several pages before moving to one of the armchairs and sitting, his bad leg extended out.

He knew not for how long he was reading when the major entered after a knock.

"Ah," he said. "Here you are. We've been searching for you."

The colonel looked up. "I am only here."

He struggled in an awkward somewhat rotating manner to get himself from the chair that had nearly swallowed him and turned to his friend. "I am sorry not to have told you."

"That's quite alright, of course. It was just that no one seemed to know where you had gone."

The colonel looked to see the page on which he was reading. There were strips of paper on a small table near the shelving on the room's left side, and he used one to mark his place, and put the volume itself on the table.

"Shall we get some exercise?" he asked, and ten minutes later he and Major Groeper were stepping down to the Brook Street pavement to do some walking in the warm summer air.

From that day on, it was understood in the house that the colonel enjoyed the solitude of a good book nestled in a comfortable chair with his bad leg outstretched. A footman would enter regularly, and there was often a cup of coffee and a biscuit or half-drunk cup of coffee and half of a biscuit on the small mahogany table that was to his right, the side away from the window.

This is how the library became the officer's sanctuary. Not even the major dared go in when the colonel was there if it could be avoided. And this might have been the end of it except that no one bothered to inform the newly arrived Catherine Bennet of this state of affairs. So several days after she herself was settled in the tumult of the Heroes Parade and Lydia and their parents had gone to Longbourn, she was curious about what was behind the closed door towards the back of the house. She spontaneously opened that door and was overwhelmed by the room's solitude and beauty. She had never ventured inside during her brief earlier stay at the house. As she looked around and up at the sculpted ceiling, her eyes drifted towards the window. There she saw a dozing figure, his book splatted on the floor and his chest rhythmically rising and falling. The slightest snore could be heard, and she took two or three steps into the room to examine him.

It was something of a shock, this soldier in a moment of complete innocence, dreaming of she could not imagine what. She wondered if he was haunted by experiences she could not contemplate. He seemed so soft and childlike. She took another step closer, but it was a step too far. It startled him and he jolted awake, spasming at the interruption.

He looked towards the window and then to his right, where he saw a frozen Catherine Bennet staring and raising her hand to her mouth as she began to back away.

"Miss Bennet is it?" he said somewhat groggily as he shook his head to rouse himself. "You must forgive me. The comforts of my cousin's library are sometimes too much to prevent me from drifting off, and I hope I did not frighten you."

"Oh, sir," she mumbled, no longer moving towards or away from him. "It is I who am deadly sorry for having interrupted your—"

"My slumber, Miss Bennet?" he said lightly.

She nodded. "Indeed, sir. Your slumber. But it shall be our secret."

He pushed himself forward so he could adjust his leg in order for him to stand.

"Please, Colonel. Do not get up on my account."

"Miss Bennet. I may be many things, but I presume to be a gentleman, and I have become quite adept at lifting myself from a chair to greet a pretty woman."

She waited, her face lit by the light streaming through the window, still frozen in place, as he repeated the movement he had perfected to get himself up from the chair. He stood awkwardly up and turned to her. He bowed in a quick motion as she curtsied in the same abbreviated fashion.

"Will you sit with me?" he asked. Softly.

"I think I had better not. I will leave you to your book." She nodded in the direction of the novel that had been so improperly allowed to fall to the floor.

He looked down at it. "Ah, Walter Scott." He looked back up to her. "I assure you, and this is no reflection of that man, but I should prefer the company of a pretty woman such as yourself."

Catherine was taken aback slightly at his second reference to her in that manner. He pointed to the twin of the chair that was his, and she went to it as he somewhat awkwardly resumed his seat with an audible grunt. She retrieved the Scott and placed it on a shelf before lowering herself to the other chair and she fell into her first conversation alone with Colonel Richard Fitzwilliam.

Happily for them both, there was one topic on which each was wildly fascinated and they were soon speaking admirably and even conspiratorially of one Elizabeth Darcy. Oh, how Catherine spoke of her older sister and how harsh she had long thought her and how she resented that Lizzy had prevented her from going north to be with Lydia and Wickham and how she would never have become what she had become, for good or for ill, without that sister.

The colonel laughed, disclosing his first meetings with Miss Elizabeth Bennet long ago at Rosings Park and how he was mesmerized by her but how they both knew for reasons of money and inclination that they were never meant to be for one another—"Like in one of my novels?" Catherine asked/said jovially—but how Darcy was in fact the only man who could possibly make her happy.

"As he has done, as I can attest."

"As can I, Miss Bennet, as can I."

The subject was hardly exhausted when there was a knock on the door. The colonel bade the interrupter come in, and one of the footmen appeared with a tray on which there was a coffee pot and a small plate containing two biscuits. When he was three or four steps in, almost precisely where Catherine had stopped who knows how recently, he halted. He stuttered.

"Begging your pardon, sir. I did not know that—"

"Miss Bennet, man."

"My apologies, sir." The footman gave a slight bow to the aforementioned Miss Bennet and said, "Miss Bennet, ma'am."

"Fear not," assured the colonel. "You are not interrupting anything but a fine conversation." He turned to Catherine. "Would you like some coffee? Tea, perhaps?"

"No, thank you, Colonel. I am due to walk with Georgiana soon, so I best get myself prepared."

The footman had not moved during this exchange, holding the small tray before himself.

When the colonel began to rise in his peculiar fashion, Catherine insisted that he remain where and as he was, and with a smile to the footman as she passed him, she was quickly out through the open door and heading up to her bedchamber to change into a dress and shoes and a bonnet appropriate for her daily turn with Georgiana Darcy.

* * * *

For whatever reason, Catherine did not think to mention her unexpected encounter with the colonel during her walk with Georgiana. And when the colonel emerged from the library—having made little headway in his Scott from the spot where he had been when the book fell to the floor—and ran into Darcy as he went to change for his own walk, his conversation with Catherine Bennet having slipped his mind as well.

The next day was warm but quite wet. The colonel and the major left the house after their early breakfast in the dining parlor of eggs, bacon, toast, and coffee. Few were out and about except those who had to be, the workers who made London operate as smoothly as it did.

The pair eschewed umbrellas, wearing wide-brimmed hats instead that did nothing to keep their gloved hands from getting wet, and they wore rain slickers and riding boots as they walked until they heard a nearby church tolling the hour, which was their signal to return to Brook Street.

For her part, when she awoke Catherine heard the battering on her window from the rain, even through her curtains, and dropped her head back on her pillow for just a few moments of additional sleep. Her mind was wandering as it had before she had drifted off the night before, and in the heat and humidity she was covered only by a thin bedsheet and wished London had the same breeze that often came through Longbourn at this time of year.

Those few moments turned far longer, and her renewed sleep was only upended when Georgiana was shaking her for her slothfulness, with a chambermaid standing in the door frame being amused by her two charges.

After fighting Georgiana off, Catherine promised that she would be arisen soon enough if she were only allowed to do so, and Georgiana gave a final giggle and turned from the room, the chambermaid stepping aside to let her through and then coming near Catherine to assist her with whatever needed assisting.

The two had agreed to breakfast together in one or the other's room. Georgiana, though, was quite hungry and took it upon herself to prompt her friend to come out. When they were finally settled, Catherine asked the housemaid who had brought up the tray with their breakfasts—light, simple fare—whether any of the gentlemen had gone out.

"Only the two officers, Miss Bennet," she said.

"In this weather?" The storm had eased somewhat, though he rain was still battering the windows.

"Oh, you know soldiers," Georgiana said. "No weather will deter *them* from doing their inspection of whatever it is they have to do in Mayfair."

Catherine looked up from her plate and out the window. Yes, it was easing, but how was the colonel's leg faring? That thought was interrupted when Georgiana asked what Catherine's plans were for the unpleasant day. Neither shopping nor visiting would be possible, at least until the early afternoon, and that only if the weather cleared.

"I should like to enjoy something to read from your brother's library," said Catherine.

"I did not know you had been in there. I meant to show it to you."

"I discovered it yesterday," Catherine said. "I found it interesting."

"Was my cousin not there?"

"The colonel? Yes, he was there. I will say I was most intimidated when I stepped in."

"Oh he thinks of it as his special place and does not like anyone to disturb him. Only a footman to refill his cup of coffee and bring another round of biscuits or a glass of claret and a plate of cheese if it is late enough in the afternoon. I do not dare go in when he is there. I should have warned you. He might have taken your head off."

Catherine thought how odd this was. She had awakened him and even for that he seemed perfectly content and gentlemanly to have her keep him company.

"But you did not mention on our walk that you had seen him," Georgiana observed.

"It was only a brief encounter. Hardly worth saying anything," Catherine said in her defense.

Georgiana huffed. "Well I suggest that if you want to read something from there, you get it now, before he comes back, just in case."

Catherine thought on this and smiled and changed the direction of the conversation by asking what Georgiana planned to do, to which Georgiana said it was a good opportunity to practice on the house's pianoforte. Thus were matters left when the ladies had finished their meal and Catherine returned to her bedchamber so she, too, could prepare for what little they had to do for the day.

Several days later, when Catherine and Elizabeth had returned from a visit to the Bingleys' on Mount Street, Lizzy went off to see to some household task while Catherine changed into a more comfortable and informal dress and a pair of inside slippers. There not being anything urgent to be done, such as writing a letter to anyone, she decided to venture down to the library. She thought it likely that the colonel would be there and could not resist the idea of disturbing him for a bit of fun. Besides, she had followed Georgiana's suggestion and taken a volume from the library before the colonel got back on that rainy day. She had finished that novel's first volume and wished to continue with the second.

"Oh," she said to the startled Colonel when she entered, without knocking. This time his book was safely in his right hand, "I had no idea anyone was here. I do beg your pardon, sir. Do not get up." This last was directed as he began the awkward dance to get from his chair. Her request fell on deaf ears as he was quickly up and quickly bowing and quickly begging that she in fact join him, said with an outstretched arm.

"I shall be a moment, Colonel," she replied, as she carried the novel's completed Part 1 to its place and pulled its neighboring Part 2 from one of the two rows of books that Lizzy had requisitioned since becoming mistress of the house, novels more suitable to a woman's taste than the volumes her husband had packed in elsewhere.

She turned, holding her book. The colonel had watched each of her movements, finding even the most mundane of them the height of grace and she feigned complete ignorance that he was doing so. "It is a novel," she advised him, pushing it slightly towards him, "that Lizzy has particularly suggested to me and I have quite enjoyed it already. Might you consider it, sir?"

She had pulled the volume back to her chest and he had not quite heard her words for her actions.

"Novel?"

"By *A Lady* to be sure."

"By *A Lady*? No, Miss Bennet, I am sure it will have no allure for me."

She smiled. "I take it upon myself the challenge of convincing you otherwise, sir."

He nodded, unable to hide his smile for *this* lady.

She said nothing as she walked to the empty chair. His good eye was very inappropriately locked on her form, a fact to which she again feigned indifference knowing full well even at her young age the universally acknowledged fact that a woman's figure appears to the greatest advantage in walking.

Her beguiling display ended when she dropped herself lightly into the chair that was the colonel's twin, doing so with quite a bit more ease than the colonel did to his. She placed her book in her lap.

"I did suspect that you might be here, Colonel. I confess it, and that I for one perhaps hoped we could renew our conversation which I found most pleasant." She held up her volume. "Or, if you prefer, I can explore my story in silence while you explore yours."

"Miss Bennet. I am at your service. I, too, found our encounter enjoyable, if I may say so. For now"—he held up his own book—"let us read while enjoying each other's company.

And with that he continued his literary journey and she resumed hers and they were both grateful for the company.

"Miss Bennet?" the colonel asked not a quarter of an hour later after he had placed his volume in his lap.

"Yes, Colonel?"

"I have noticed how quickly you seem to be devouring that book."

"It was recommended to me by my sister." She held it up in her left hand. "You might like it. Two very different sisters with a scant inheritance and less hope. I find that few journeys are more pleasant than one taken in a good book. But I doubt you would have any interest in this particular one."

"You might be surprised at what an old soldier living for long periods with little to do but drill in isolated camps would find of interest. I will confess one cannot surpass Scott in such things, though I daresay he would not fit in with your *womanly* mind."

"Womanly mind Colonel?"

"Your sister confessed to the acknowledged—shall we say?—inadequacies of the education provided to you Bennet girls."

"Lizzy?"

"Indeed. It was when I met her while Darcy and I were visiting his aunt, Lady Catherine—"

"Who came to us in Hertfordshire and proceeded to insult our parents."

"I once heard that, but I cannot speak to it. I will say, however, that my aunt was very rude to Lizzy when we were at Rosings Park and asked her the most inappropriate questions."

"Including about the education we received, which I admit was not very much and I do now regret that."

"As I was destined to be a soldier, I fear that I did not get as broad an education as Darcy and my brother did. So you and I"—he lifted his own tome to her—"are on somewhat the same footing in terms of trying to improve ourselves by taking advantage of my cousin's superb library."

And they resumed their reading and thus matters continued for a period until there was a knock on the door and its being opened revealed Elizabeth.

"I've been looking for you," she said somewhat crossly to be sure to Catherine, "and did not expect you be disturbing Colonel Fitzwilliam." She curtsied to him and insisted that he not get up. She reminded Catherine of their agreement to go for a walk and that it was past time to get started.

Catherine apologized to Elizabeth for being so tardy and to the colonel for having to leave him so abruptly. When they were gone, and particularly when Catherine was gone, the colonel found himself disappointed. He had little time to dwell on his loss, as the major was soon upon him with a reminder that they, too, had planned on taking their own regular turn. And so they too were soon on the Mayfair pavement. Again, Catherine Bennet's name was not mentioned.

Within the week, Catherine and the colonel were near constant companions in the library, alternating between reading and conversing and falling into the most pleasant of days, even, or especially, on those with the angriest weather. It was enough for them both to forget the wounds that the officer had suffered, at least until he got up from his seat.

One day, though, the colonel again seemed to bristle at Catherine's midday appearance. She at first ignored it but she knew something was bothering him. She closed the third volume of her novel.

"I know you think of me as something of a child, barely a year older than Georgiana. But I am not a child, I assure you, and I will listen to you whenever you wish to speak in confidence even though I have scant experience of the world, especially of *your* world."

She moved her hands towards him but only slightly. He refused to speak of the anxiousness he had had about his future so he ignored this motion. She held fast.

"That is all I wish to say." She placed her book on the small table beside her chair. It was a clear day.

"Now, sir, I must try to get some walking in. Will you be kind enough to accompany me, at least to the yard?"

"If you give me time to change, I will be pleased to walk with you."

She told Lizzy of her plan and of his and the pair for the first time ventured together in the still London air. In the days that followed, the portion of time spent reading in the library and the portion of time spent conversing, which had earlier been well in favor of the reading side of the ledger, was chiefly in favor of the latter.

An understanding was reached between the two on several points.

First, he conceded her point that it was tiresome that they being related in a manner she would address him as "Colonel" and he would address her as "Miss Bennet." So these were converted to "Richard" and "Catherine," respectively. "Not *Kitty*?" he asked when she told him her preference. "It was always Kitty and usually Lydia and Kitty," she said, "and I do not believe I am that girl anymore."

"So," he said good-naturedly, "*Catherine* it shall be."

Second, each was free to interrupt the other within reason, to share a passage here or a passage there.

Third, they would interrupt their own reading when the footman came with a tray, bearing coffee for him, tea for her, and biscuits for them both and simply converse.

Finally, if the weather permitted it, they would end their session with a stroll on the pavement, the length based on how the colonel's left leg felt on the day.

Of course Elizabeth soon caught on to all of this. She kept it to herself, even at first from Darcy, to see where whatever it was might be headed, although she had a pretty good idea what it was and was optimistic about where that might be.

20

As to the major and Georgiana, they did not notice these goings on. Their attentions were elsewhere. In particular near one of the two Broadwood grand pianofortes that Darcy had bought. One had been shipped to Pemberley. The other was acquired for when Georgiana was coming to town. It was made in London. She had suggested that it be placed in a non-conspicuous spot. Her brother would not hear of it.

Thus it sat majestically and prominently in a corner of Brook Street's great drawing room, positioned so that it could be rotated for use as a performance instrument for guests.

From the moment she touched its shiny ivory and ebony keys and played several major, minor, and melodic scales from left to right and from right to left, she was in love with it. The touch. The sound. The feel. It was a superb instrument.

Georgiana was confident in her musical ability but remained otherwise shy. It had taken her some days after settling into Brook Street to feel at home at the Broadwood. She still refrained from playing it when others were about unless either her brother or, more likely, her sister-in-law insisted she perform.

Darcy had told his sister about *Elizabeth's* playing at Rosings Park. It was, he said, not as technically adept as it might have been but was extremely pleasant to hear. He did not mention that he had discussed this at Lady Catherine's and how she had admitted to a lack of practice having limited her playing. Nor did he mention how he was cut when she added that *he* might himself benefit were he to practice his skills in society as she might benefit by practicing her skills at a keyboard.

Darcy sometimes insisted that his wife *sing for her supper*, and thus the two reluctant musicians, his sister and his wife, at times were compelled to perform one Mozart or Beethoven piece or another before the visitors on a particular evening. Georgiana far more enjoyed sitting alone on the bench with music before her for hours at a time in the afternoon, letting her fingers dance across the keys.

And as had happened when Catherine entered the library that day when the colonel had fallen asleep, the major happened to enter the drawing room while Georgiana played.

Georgiana did not at first notice him. He had heard her from the hallway. It sounded soothing and familiar, though he did not know what it was, and he could not help but slowly and quietly open the door. The Beethoven—which is what it was—floated from near the window, and the tall woman's cream-colored dress sprinkled with flowers caught the light very fetchingly, and in contrast to the rosewood of the instrument.

She had moved from the sleepiness of the sonata's first movement to the muscular and brutal staccato of the second, oblivious to all the world. He took only a few steps in before halting. He would not interrupt her for the world, lest she stop playing what was dancing and floating about the room. He had some familiarity with such music but this was something sublime to him in how she was playing it.

When she finished one section, she paused to reach and turn to a new page. He coughed. It startled her. Her back stiffened, and she looked at him very crossly.

"I beg pardon, Miss Darcy. I could not—"taking several steps closer—"resist when I heard your playing as I passed by. Please excuse me."

He bowed. She pushed the bench slightly with the backs of her legs as she turned to curtsey to him. She did not know whether to forgive him his trespass!

"Might I help with your page turning?" he quietly and spontaneously asked.

She looked at the page on the stand on the pianoforte and then back at him.

"It would be a great help, Major, if it's no bother and if you can weather the storm I sometimes make of this piece."

Without another word, he went to her. He moved the bench slightly to the right so they could sit together.

"Do you read music, Major?" she asked.

"I fear that I was not so tutored, Miss Bennet."

"Then please try to follow along as best you can and I shall nod my head when it is time. *Do you understand?*"

"I think I do. I will do my best."

"I'm sure you will," said she, and with that her focus was again on the music and the quarter and dotted eighth notes and the ties and the other musical notations that he could not make out hard as he tried to keep track of it. He was completely at sea, his eyes tight on her profile until he saw her nod. He fumbled for the score and managed to turn the page and it seemed to him at least that she had not missed a beat.

By the time she had finished the piece with two more relatively successful turns, their thighs had come together. When she lifted her hands in some satisfaction, he briskly slid away from her. Pretending that this *innocent* touching had not occurred, after a cough, she asked whether he was tired and bored. He insisted he was neither. She smiled at her helper.

"Alas, dear major. I have had quite enough of Herr Beethoven for one afternoon. Shall I ring for some refreshments?"

He squeezed from the bench and she pushed it back with her legs and went to the wall and pulled the cord next to the window. A footman was quickly with them, surprised to see that Miss Darcy was not alone.

"I will have some tea. And you, major?" She looked at her new assistant. He said that would be more than acceptable to him, even most pleasant, and with a bow the footman was gone to fetch the things from the kitchen and Miss Darcy asked Major Groeper to sit with her by the front window while they awaited his return. And when they sat they spoke for some time.

*   *   *   *

As tended to happen in London, when Catherine awoke several days later, it was again raining. She was preparing herself to go to breakfast with Georgiana when that lady knocked on her door and came straight in. Breakfast was set up in Georgiana's room and she pulled her friend there. Before they could discuss what they intended to do for the day, Georgiana said, "I know the colonel and the major are out there now, but I will not do that myself."

"Nor will I," agreed Catherine.

"Then, I think I might practice on the pianoforte, if you do not object my dear."

"I will not object. I might pick up a novel I am reading and make myself comfortable in the library for the morning," Catherine said.

"What of the colonel?" Georgiana asked.

"Well, as you say, he and the major will be out—"

"Yes, but they will return."

"Then the colonel will simply have to tolerate my presence if he wishes to use the library. That is all I can say about it," Catherine said, standing to prove her determination on the point.

"Well, Catherine, I cannot say that the major will be coming in to interrupt me while I am playing, but if he does, I will ignore him and continue to play whether he likes it or not!"

"You are a cruel woman, Georgiana Darcy, to ignore such a man should he chance to enter the drawing room while you are amusing yourself."

"And you, Miss Catherine Bennet, are similarly cruel to occupy the poor Colonel's refuge by reading some flight of fancy that Lizzy suggested to you."

"It is quite an interesting flight," Catherine countered. "I think you should read it as it might put some sense into a silly girl like you."

With the idea of having won, Catherine vacated her friend's bedchamber, and Georgiana was content to allow her friend her moment to believe she had her brief triumph as she finished her tea and a pastry alone and wondered whether the major would dare interrupt her playing.

21.

While these matters were taking place chiefly within the walls of the Darcy house on Brook Street, the colonel's rehabilitation was progressing outside as well. Word of the presence of this cavalryman injured at Waterloo and with a trusted aide had reached the nearby stable. At first, the two officers walked there with Darcy and Bingley. All but the colonel would find their mounts and take turns in Hyde Park. He would follow slowly on foot with his walking stick. When he arrived, he would take up a fine position on a bench to watch his friends and the other riders pass.

It pained him that he could not ride, to simply climb aboard one of the horses at the stable and see what would happen. He resisted the temptation. He was seeing a Harley Street doctor regularly, and the opinion was more and more optimistic that the expected date was not far off.

If the sun was out and bright, he made sure to sit so it faced him and he allowed it to wash across his face and warm it and perhaps let his mind wander to pleasant memories, which were more and more drifting to one Catherine Bennet.

Some weeks later the doctor said he could chance it. "No galloping," he was told, and he promised that that was the last thing on his mind. Whatever the validity of his intentions, when he was at last aboard one of the finer stallions, under the watchful eyes of his friends and all the others in the stable, all his nerves and a goodly portion of sense were gone. They had reached the park at a canter. Then he, and his mount, was in his milieu. His legs, however weakened by French artillery, grabbed control of the beast in its first strides. There was nothing tentative or careful about it. He and the brown chestnut were as one, moving away from all but the major, who spurred his own horse to match the colonel's until good sense prevailed and they slowed with the awed Darcy and Bingley able to catch them up.

Atlas, the colonel's favorite, had been lost during the battle, as had so many others. His body had—he imagined—rotted for some days until it and those of the scores and hundreds of other horses and mules and men were put to the torch as the only means of clearing away the war's debris. But the colonel himself had lived to ride another day, as the battlefield surgeon Mr. Reynolds said he would. For the first time since he raced into the French infantry, he felt whole again.

There was not room in the park for what he was doing, and it was flatly prohibited and went completely against the promise he had made to his doctor. But Colonel Fitzwilliam was no amateur looking to impress some lady or embarrass some rival. Neither he nor the horse had a moment of doubt as he rode past and through the other horses smooth as silk, with only the major able to follow.

It did not last long. The colonel was not in true shape to ride that way for long. And the excitement soon gave way to appreciating the danger that such riding posed for himself and others. Still, it was enough. He had ridden again!

"Now," he said to the others as they rode easily back to the stable at a canter outside the Park, "I am ready," he said as he patted the side of the heated stallion's head, "to go to Pemberley."

After six weeks, there was barely a trace of injury on the colonel. He wore a patch, but his leg was almost fully healed, and he could walk, albeit still with difficulty and a pronounced limp but more and more without a cane.

Increasingly, though, those walks were with Catherine.

22

As the day when the residents of the two London houses would venture to the north neared, Catherine sat with Elizabeth in Mrs. Darcy's simple but fine study. "What do you think of the colonel?" she asked.

The two were in a pair of comfortable chairs in the corner. It was a rainy Tuesday, and it did not appear that the sun would be seen for some time. Georgiana was with them at first, but she excused herself when she realized the conversation between the others was drifting into sisterly territory. While moments like these always affected the sisterless Georgiana, she loved Elizabeth and Catherine and never resented their natural bonds.

The Bennets were out of the hearing of the footmen who stood like statues near the front window when Catherine asked about the colonel. Elizabeth quickly recovered.

"Do you have some affectionate thoughts towards him?" she asked.

"I cannot say, exactly. I look forward to seeing him and regret it when he leaves. I think of him when I am trying to sleep and I hope he will come to me in a dream, although he never has."

"I should not put much credence in who is or is not in your dreams."

"Did Darcy appear in yours? Before you married him?"

"Darcy! Goodness, no. Which may prove that the presence or absence of a man in a woman's dreams is of no significance. But the conscious thoughts sent in his direction? That is a far different thing."

Catherine sat back in her chair and her shoulders slouched.

"If that is the case, Lizzy, I believe I may have some affection for him." She laughed and fled the room.

Elizabeth had long been fond of her husband's cousin though she had never had a *woman's* affection for him. Plainly things were different with Catherine, however much she tried to hide it. *Was there a prospect of affection and even love developing between them?*

Jane had endorsed the suggestion when Lizzy brought it up with her. Though the thoughts of the eldest Bennet, and of Mary, were increasingly devoted to what was growing inside Jane.

Elizabeth was astonished when her husband himself raised the matter of Catherine and the colonel. Although they each had their own bedchamber, he often stayed in her bed for some time after they were intimate. Both cherished those moments when they lay naked beside one another by the light of just one or two withering candles and under a blanket. Each could give rein to the almost random thoughts that flickered within them.

"I have come to be fond of your sister Catherine," he told her. This was when Catherine had been back at the house for over a fortnight. "Do you think she might have developed a fondness for my cousin?"

They were on their sides, his arms gently around her, his voice brushing against her ear.

"You have become quite the observant one," she said vaguely as she savoured his grip. "Yes, my dear, it has become apparent that there may be something growing between the two."

"Growing?"

"Indeed. At first I thought it was a kindness that has developed more and more since Catherine is out from under Lydia's influence. A maturity in her. A desire to care, actually *care* for another."

"How do you mean?"

"I doubt he likes or even realizes it, but she is always doing little things to and for him. Slight but almost intimate."

"And now?"

"And now I think it far more womanly, far more than a desire to tend to him as damaged. I believe it may be more, maybe even much more. At first I thought she looked at him like a girl might look at a puppy that has injured its paw and was hobbling around the farmyard."

"But of course he is not a puppy and she is not a farmgirl."

"No, but the essential kindness of the woman she has grown into cannot be denied and I was afraid that her attentions were along those instinctive lines than otherwise."

She turned half around so they could face each other.

"I think she may have fallen in love."

"You truly believe it has become so advanced?" he asked.

"On her part, I believe it truly has. Consider the evidence."

And they mentioned the time they devoted to one another, the simple acts of keeping near each other even if they were not particularly engaged. Their walks.

Elizabeth laughed.

"You will not recall, I think, but I was a fool not to appreciate the meaning of how frequently you *happened* upon me on my strolls at Rosings Park that...interesting time at your aunt's."

"You really suspected me of doing something...underhanded. I thought I had well cloaked my desire to see you." He smiled before kissing her on the forehead.

"It was so long ago, and the memory is clearer in the passage of time. I have no doubt that our two relations are largely oblivious to what is happening between them, or each at least believes he or she is keeping it hidden."

"Is that not the way of love?" Darcy concluded.

Two or three days later, however, the two subjects of the Darcys' discussion found themselves taking a turn along the pavement towards Grosvenor Square. It was not a matter of happenstance. The household would be heading from town early the next morning and the colonel would be separated from Catherine for some time, she continuing to Pemberley and he to Haverford Hall with Major Groeper. This separation had clouded the minds of each of them as the day approached. When the colonel suggested the walk on the eve of the move, Catherine readily agreed.

As it was a chilled but not cold day, they each wore a light coat. Steps from the house itself, she placed her arm through his, and he nearly unconsciously grasped her hand, his walking stick keeping rhythm with their steps. It was quite as intimate as they two had ever been, made even more so when she realized her head was leaning against his arm.

"I have enjoyed our time together, Miss Bennet."

"Miss Bennet?" she said mockingly.

He smiled. "My Catherine. I do not know that I would have come through this nearly so well without you."

"Me, Richard?" She was touched by his words but did not believe that she had the slightest to do with his recovery. After all, she had done little but keep him company. She was genuinely surprised.

They were on the path in the Square, just one of a number of pairs of couples taking advantage of what was a brisk air before most would also be heading from town. Whether they were closer to one another than were any of the long-married pairs or even the young-married pairs of lovers could not be said. He with his military bearing and slight limp, helped by the casual-appearing swinging of his stick. She in a fashionable bonnet and dress and coat and shoes.

"Would you…" he began but paused.

They were quiet for several steps, a silence she could not resist for long. "Would I what?"

"Shall we sit?" he said, nodding toward one of a series of benches that lined the pavement. Their arms became disengaged and they sat near but not close to one another.

"Would you consider it inappropriate were I to engage in a correspondence with you, perhaps through your sister, while you are at Pemberley?"

Here, a man who had charged without fear into the heart of the French infantry only months earlier was irresolute in posing this simple request. *Would you consider it inappropriate where I to engage in a correspondence with you while you are at Pemberley?*

"I think I would enjoy that," she said. "And you will allow me to write to you?"

They then got up to continue their stroll and head back to Brook Street to prepare for their impending departure to the north of England.

23

The routine at the Darcy house on Brook Street soon ended. Most of London—at least that very small portion of London that could afford it—had already left for the country. The Darcys and the Bingleys had delayed their own departures until the colonel had had some time to recover. Lady Catherine had written to the colonel to express her *fondest wish* that he spend the season in Kent. In a prompt response, he begged for her forgiveness. He was going instead to Pemberley and near his family's estate, Haverford House.

"When I return to town, dear Aunt," he wrote, "I shall be sure to spend some time with you and my cousin at Rosings, as I have so pleasantly in the past."

On a Wednesday in mid-September, at around Michaelmas, carriages were loaded up and the journey north began. The group consisted of nine with a number of servants occupying two additional carriages.

The passengers regularly exchanged places at the periodic stops for changes of horses, meals, and overnight stays.

The travel was slow but enjoyable as the weather remained favorable except for a brief period each afternoon when a passing storm offered a welcome change for the travelers, if not for the coachmen, footmen, or, perhaps, horses.

Then late on the afternoon of the third day, they reached Nottingham. The two officers would continue to Waddington in a hired coach while the others continued to Pemberley.

And so it was that the colonel was finally off to be reunited with his parents for the first time since he abruptly left Lincolnshire after Bonaparte's shocking escape from Elba.

The colonel and the major were only a few miles on a smooth stretch of road north of Nottingham and falling into the rhythm of the carriage when the latter spoke after several false starts.

"Tell me, sir," he began with a feigned nonchalance, "but does your cousin Miss Georgiana have any engagements or potential engagements?"

The question roused the colonel, whose mind was drifting with thoughts of what his parents would think when they at last saw him, far more real than he made himself in the correspondence that he had regularly sent to them since he had arrived in London.

"My cousin?" the colonel was able to respond.

"Yes, sir. Does she, if you should happen to know, have an...interest in anyone? Or does anyone, if you know, sir, have an interest in her?"

He looked at his companion in quite a different way and could not conceal a smile. He had been so enchanted by Catherine that he had failed to pay attention to what the major was doing while he was visiting Brook Street. "I should think that Darcy would be better able to answer you, my friend, but I do not know if either he or I would necessarily be privy to any such thing."

"I understand, sir. I only inquire about the scope of your *actual* knowledge."

"On that, then, I can only say that I am unaware of anything in either direction." He paused. "I must tell you—" he began but stopped.

"Tell me what, sir?"

"It is nothing, Major. Nothing at all. I have been much abroad, as you know, but I can say that neither she nor her brother has given me even the suggestion of anything in that regard. After all, she is not out as yet and no one in town at least would dare act as if she were. While she would be unlikely to disclose any *informal* prospects herself to me, she would surely have told her brother and I believe he would tell me, which he has not. I think you can safely conclude that the field is open to you. Or at the least I can say that it is not *closed* to you."

The major had sufficient dealings with Georgiana that he had formulated an opinion of her. The colonel would let him woo her and perhaps even win her in his own fashion. He would not stand in his way.

It was suddenly apparent that the still waters of Major Michael Groeper may have run very deep after all. And the thought led him to think how he might do his own bit of wooing for one of the other ladies they had so recently left in Nottingham.

24.

With the roads for the most part in good condition, the two officers reached Haverford House in the late afternoon. A letter had been dispatched from London predicting when they would arrive, and it proved quite accurate. Even before the carriage rolled to a halt in the drive in front of the great house, a footman was ready to open its door and his parents, Lord and Lady Waddington, were emerging.

Since he was back in England after the great battle, he had tried to send them a letter whenever he sent one to Darcy, though the ones to his parents were somewhat shorter and less detailed, particularly concerning the colonel's physical condition. He had disclosed the loss of his left eye and the injury to his left leg. "My appearance beyond that," he wrote, "has suffered some scarring but in all events I do not think I am too horribly affected."

When they were on the ground and both his parents had finished eyeing their son and confirming that he was damaged but not broken, his father stepped to shake his son's hand most vehemently and his mother threw her arms around her son and he reciprocated with her. Neither of his parents were by nature or position prone to flights of emotion, but that did not matter now that their son had returned alive from the horrors they had read so much about.

"The village will be greatly disappointed with you, son, if you do not venture there in the morning. You've been the talk of the place ever since word of your...injuries reached us."

The colonel laughed. "It seemed more than a few were waiting for us and many waved as we passed them by."

"They are good people, son, and so very proud of you."

"Father, were many others in the village affected?"

"Many a good lad joined up, you know, and a few of them, well, a few of them are not coming back. But most folks have had word from their boys and men that they made it through, some better than others, and some have made it home."

The colonel extended his arm out towards his companion.

"Father, mother, please forgive me. This is Major Michael Groeper who has long been my most cherished aide and confidant. I should not have made it home half so well had he not been with me on the field and nearly every moment since."

The major bowed to the lord and lady.

"And we understand that you were in the battle, Major," said Lady Waddington.

"I was, m'lady."

"In the battle?" the colonel interrupted as he slapped the other officer on the back. "He went in with me and the rest and after I was knocked out"—the colonel had included a truncated report on the battle in a letter he wrote his father from London—"he and the rest who could went back again and again. If it were not for them, I hate to think what would have become of us. But as I say, he took care of me from the moment the French were done for. Every step of the way."

The lady now interrupted.

"You must be tired after your journey. I think we should go inside," and the group adjourned into the house.

"Major," she said, "a room has been prepared for you next to our son's. We hope it will be agreeable to you."

"Oh, Lady Waddington, I assure you, a bed with a roof over it and some blankets is a paradise to me."

"Well," Lord Waddington said, "I like to think we can provide something more than that, especially for one as welcome here as you are."

With that, the men began to follow a footman to their rooms. Lord Waddington reached for the major's arm to delay him.

"We know what you have done for our son, Major. You have our eternal gratitude."

"Thank you, m'lord. I consider myself his friend, but I was in fact doing my duty as any officer in our King's service would do."

"But which you did," Lady Waddington said, and with a bow, the major thanked them and quickly caught up to the colonel so they could get comfortable in their rooms before dinner.

*　*　*　*

There was still light enough when the two were settled for them to venture to the estate's stables. One reached them down a slightly winding path. They contained two rows of stalls that were very well tended to. When the stablemaster saw the two coming, he rushed to greet the colonel, proud as could be that one of the house had done everyone so proud as a cavalryman. The colonel introduced Major Groeper.

The stablemaster was well aware that the colonel's favorite, Atlas, who he knew as a rambunctious colt, was struck down in the battle. It was the way of the life, but was still sad, and the stablemaster had been keeping an eye out for a horse of comparable merit. He found one, and he hoped the stallion would meet with the colonel's approval. There was a second, quite comparable mare. He hoped the major would find her to his liking during his stay.

The two horses were in adjoining stalls near the main door. It was too late for them to be taken out, but the *introductions* went well after which the men returned to the house for an informal dinner with the Lord and Lady.

The next morning, soon after the sun was up, following a pleasant evening, the officers had breakfast. They were sufficiently excited about getting out that they ventured into the kitchen itself—into the kitchen itself!—for their meal, much to the discomfort, it must be said, of Cook and the balance of the kitchen staff.

The intrusion was tolerated and the two men, sated by their eggs and toast and bacon with heaps of coffee, were off and out for their riding.

They made short work of getting the stallion and the mare prepared and within thirty minutes of leaving the house, the two were in their saddles and heading briskly towards the village itself.

"My father says we are expected," said the colonel, "and we shall not disappoint." With that, they briskly covered the over two miles or so to Waddington Village and those who saw them, mostly out in the fields, waved their arms or hats and hurrahed as they passed.

Waddington Village was due south of Lincoln. The road to Sleaford passed just to the east, and a pair of streets extended from that road to the west. They and a north-south road that crossed them both until it veered east to connect with the post road defined the village. It had rows of shops and an inn, a tavern, and a stable. The great house itself was some two miles as the crow flies to the southwest on a slight hill that offered a view of the steeple and the taller parts of the village.

The two officers rode slowly through before exiting and allowing their horses full rein, the colonel leading and feeling more comfortable—more *natural*—with each of his mount's graceful strides as they circled back on various trails and roads until they reached a prominent hill to the northwest of the great house. They dismounted and left their horses to graze as they looked across the valley. As with the house, this vista gave them a view of some of the larger buildings in the village and the church itself.

"This is a place a boy could spend hours," the colonel said. He led Groeper to a natural cluster of rocks that offered a fine vantage point. It is where they sat.

The colonel interrupted the quiet, "Even in winter, with the trees bare, it offered a glimmer of something grander than my little world."

"Very different from where a London boy might find a place to sit," Groeper said.

"Different, yes. But a place to dream is a place to dream, do not you think?"

"Well for me," the major answered, "watching the people and horses and carriages pass was my view, and I ca not say it was so bad."

They looked out for a period until the colonel spoke.

"I am sometimes torn between life in the country and life in the city. I've often felt wistful about the city when I am in the country and *vice versa*. In some respects, though, the choice is not entirely mine."

"What do you mean, if I may be so forward?"

"I have my commission, which is of little use to me now and must soon be surrendered," the colonel said, not turning from the view. "I must think of what is to become of me and how I am to afford it."

He was silent for a moment, using his hand to shield his eyes from the sun as he gazed across the valley.

Groeper interrupted. "One of the blessings of being a city lawyer's son is that one does not become accustomed to a view such as this or rooms such as the one your parents have allotted to me here. I fear they, and you, may be spoiling me."

"You are too old and have been through too much," disagreed the colonel, "to allow a fleeting visit to a great house that is very cold in the winter to alter your character. No, Groeper, you do have an advantage in that respect. I cannot say the same."

He paused a moment.

"Of course, you will become accustomed to such a life should you win Georgiana Darcy."

The name had not been mentioned since the prior day, when the two were alone in the carriage. But it had been uppermost in the major's mind and was surprisingly high in the colonel's.

"Can you think that is why I have thought of her?"

"I do not think that. I know you too well. But others will."

"Including her brother?" asked the major.

"I cannot be sure of that. He will be suspicious. He is very protective of her, with good reason. But you have comported yourself quite well and I, as I said, will vouch for the fact that what he has seen is a display of your true character. Others who do not know you will think otherwise but—"

He looked over at his colleague awkwardly with his one eye. "But what is that to you?"

The major was again relieved. In this he thought himself far different from the colonel. He could never debate the merits of the country versus the city. He might savor his visits to the former but could not imagine living anywhere but the latter. And yet his too brief encounters with Miss Georgiana Darcy made him wonder. Whether he could or would do that if it was made a condition of their marriage. *Marriage?* He had not allowed himself to dare think of her in that way. But now it could not be avoided.

He began to consider whether *she* could be content in the simple life he had long expected himself to lead. The sort of simple life his parents engaged in in their modest house in Cheapside. Nothing so opulent and servant laded as the city houses, most particularly the Darcys' house, he visited in Mayfair.

"You can only get so far without Darcy's approval," the colonel interrupted the major's thoughts. "He knows she is wealthy and that she will attract much interest, as I am sure she has done already. He will not give her up easily. Nor will I, as her other guardian. I assure you, Groeper, that neither of us will judge a man, at least for his sister, by the size of his wallet." He again looked out to the south towards the village.

"I cannot say that you have the field to yourself, but you have every opportunity to make your case if you are serious about her. You have only just met her, you know."

"I do know, and I will not be such a fool as to suggest that I am certain of my affections for her."

"What about the other one, Catherine Bennet?" asked the colonel.

"Her? She seems pleasant enough and she is surely handsome enough. She does seem close to Miss Darcy. I see nothing particularly special about her."

"You do not?"

"No. I do feel there is something *special* about Miss Darcy. What it is and what it becomes, I cannot say. But I would like to explore it."

The colonel appreciated this honesty. Glad, frankly, that his friend had been unable to see, let alone appreciate, Catherine's specialness, leaving *that* field open to him. He thought it peculiar though, and perhaps because of his intimate relationship with Georgiana as almost a sister—since Darcy was more a father than a brother to her—he would never see his cousin in the light of a potential lover.

As their stiffness made them rise from the rock on which they had never gotten quite comfortable, the colonel told Groeper that if he decided to embark on a campaign to woo and ultimately *win* Georgiana Darcy, he would be an ally.

*   *   *   *

The two officers quickly settled into life at Haverford House. They rode twice a day, without regard to the weather, and the earl sometimes joined them for some less strenuous rides around the estate. The colonel and the major also made a point of venturing into Waddington Village several times and having their midday meal at the tavern there.

During one of those meals, the colonel asked Groeper if he remembered the request that should the colonel expire during the battle he would make sure to deliver by hand a letter to his cousin.

"Of course, sir. Thank God I did not have to."

The colonel nodded. "Yes, thank God." He took a drink of ale from his stein. "I have left it in my trunk and confirmed that it was still there when we reached London and now that we have reached here. I am telling you this for the same reason, that it should still be delivered to Darcy even if I die simply by breaking my neck in a fall from my horse."

Now it was the major who took to his ale.

"So I wish you to know that. I entrust you with that task. I believe now that we are here that I must tell you the secret of my letter and why it is so important that Darcy know it."

He lifted his stein and finished what remained of his ale and got up. The major echoed the action with his own stein and followed the colonel to the bar, where he paid the bill and wished the proprietor and the others a fond goodbye.

Once they were outside and a groom brought their rested horses to them, they headed south until they traveled about one mile from the village. There the colonel slowed and the two rode past a farmstead. The colonel's eyes surveyed the place like a scout and seeing nothing he resumed their pace until they were well clear. He reined in his horse till he stopped and then leapt to the ground. The major followed.

"My secret is at that farmhouse we passed."

"The one where you were looking for someone or something?"

"For someone, but I did not see anyone."

"Who were you looking for?"

"My son."

The major froze for a moment until he could recover his senses. Before he could speak, though, the colonel resumed.

"The letter I wrote to Darcy told him. I did not know about it...about *him*...until I was last here. The mother came to me discreetly and asked me to visit her and when I did she reminded me of an...incident some ten years ago, before I first left Waddington for the army. I will spare you the details, but the result of our rendezvous was a son. Again I knew nothing of it...Of him. She was soon to be married and she told me years later that her husband believes the boy to be his. No one knows, she said. No one doubts that fiction.

"I asked her what she wanted, and she said she, her husband, and the boy were quite content in their lives. It is not an easy life, of course, but it was *their* life, she said."

"So why did she tell you? Did you have any inkling?"

"I did not. I was gone soon after our liaison and had not seen or spoken to her since. I confess not to being particularly interested in the village's and the villagers' affairs."

The two had wrapped their horses' reins around a tree and were sitting on a stone wall that ran along the side of the road, separating the road from a wheat field that was near being harvested.

"She said that she realized that I was going into harm's way and things would be very dangerous and she thought she owed it to me to tell me that I had a son. She claimed it was as simple as that. *You should know, Colonel, that you have a fine boy as you go back to war.* That's what she said."

"She did not ask for anything?"

"If I gave her anything and exposed what she and I had done and that she had kept the secret and deceived her husband all these years—she said he was their only child and the brightest thing to ever have happened to her husband—it would destroy everyone, not least the boy. I believed her in this.

"But I cannot ignore that there is a boy of whom I am the father. I cannot ignore my obligations."

The colonel's voice continued in its flat manner. It was not clear to whom he was speaking.

"I must do something for him, of course, provided there is no danger of my relationship with the boy becoming known. Not for me, as I said, but for the boy and his mother and, I think, the man who everyone else believes is the father."

"And what is that to be?"

"I cannot say. But it will be *something*. I felt it necessary now that we are in the country not a mile from their house that you know the truth so that you can inform my cousin. That he can do something for the boy, be it as simple as offering him a living and arranged for a period at Cambridge if the lad has leanings in that direction or arranging for some sort of clerkship if his mind goes towards the law.

"How that can be done without her husband or anyone else, especially the boy, knowing, I cannot say either."

With that, the colonel rose.

"I did not mean to burden you, my friend. I felt it was necessary."

"I understand, sir."

They were undoing their horses as they said this and when in their saddles and turning away from that house at a trot but in a direction that would get them back to Haverford House, the colonel said, "I trust you do, Major. I trust that you do know that, my friend."

25

Darcy had extended an invitation to the two officers to visit Pemberley for a fortnight or so as the weather permitted, and the pair rode to that great house in late November. It happened that while the colonel was aware of his colleague's interest in Georgiana, his colleague was seemingly ignorant of the colonel's interest in Catherine.

Once in Derbyshire, the two, often with Darcy and Bingley, spent many an hour riding and even racing around the Pemberley Woods. As they had in Waddington, they became regulars for their midday meal at the tavern in Lambton, five miles from Pemberley itself. With each ride, it was apparent that the colonel's strength was returned and that except for the permanent damages, most notably the lost eye but the injured leg as well, he was much as he had always been.

When the gentlemen returned from a ride, the ladies, that being Georgiana and all of the Bennet girls but Lydia—who was happily back in Newcastle with her husband awaiting word of what was to become of them when the army was broken up—would have already eaten and were strolling the grounds, sitting doing needlepoint or reading, in Elizabeth's own parlor on the second floor, or going by chaise into Lambton for a stroll among the shops.

Lambton was not unlike Meryton in this regard, and the ladies became familiar figures alighting from their carriage and walking up and down the town's slight high street. By this time, great deference was accorded Jane, whose belly was very round. Darcy had arranged for one of Sheffield's most respected physicians to visit at least once every fortnight to ensure that things were progressing as they should. Which they were.

With each passing day, Mary tended more and more to Jane, to such an extent that Elizabeth felt some pain for her own displacement.

In any case, the house's Broadwood pianoforte was the equal of the one in London, the one on which Georgiana and her *assistant* Major Groeper found themselves sitting closer to one another with each session. In Derbyshire, he was immediately known as Michael to her, and he had picked up enough about musical notation to have become adept at turning the pages of her scores precisely when she required them be turned. It was as if they had never been separated.

While those two had scant interest in the fine library, which, as we have noted (and as Caroline Bingley herself had once testified to), was among the finest in the country, the same could not be said for the colonel and Miss Catherine Bennet.

And so matters stood among them.

As a rule, the group—excepting the colonel and Major Groeper—went to the small church in Lambton for services. But several Sundays after their arrival, Darcy suggested that they instead go to Kympton. This was a parish whose living Darcy controlled as part of his estate. It was the living that George Wickham had expected to get when it became vacant until he sold his entitlement for three thousand pounds after Darcy's father died.

John Roberts was the parson who was granted the living after several lean years as a roaming and underpaid curate in the livings of more fortunate clergymen. He was a man in his mid-thirties with, at the time of taking it, a wife and two children. He was more academically inclined than were many such clergyman and he had the particular advantage of having been at

Cambridge when Darcy and Wickham were students there.

Roberts's wife had passed suddenly just over a year before of consumption, and the care of the parson and his children was taken over by one of the older widows in Kympton.

Darcy did not know this latter bit when he thought to take those staying at the house to Kympton. They arrived in a pair of Pemberley carriages fifteen minutes before services. Roberts stood in front of the modest church greeting parishioners when they did. He immediately recognized his patron when he saw the group coming from the carriages but after a bow of recognition continued with his greetings of the parishioners until Darcy and the rest were upon them.

"Mr. Darcy. It is an honor to have you here, sir," he said to the gentleman he first knew at Cambridge and with whom he had a comfortable interview before being offered the living. The greeting was loud enough for word of the great man's attendance to spread to all the nearby parishioners.

Darcy was somewhat taken aback by the attention, but Elizabeth was quick enough to introduce herself and her sisters and Georgiana and Bingley, the others in their party.

By tradition, the front pew was left vacant for the benefactor of the Parish, and word spread quickly among those already in the church that Mr. Darcy himself was in attendance. As he entered with his entourage, the entirety of those there stood, much to the embarrassment of Darcy and the others, until they themselves were seated.

This might have been a simple and mundane episode in our story but for the fact that the entourage included Miss Mary Bennet. Since she had convinced Lizzy and

Jane to allow her to leave Longbourn and become part of the Bingley house, she had quieted some of her more strident views and tempered some of her more strident behavior and had become close to Jane as Catherine had to Elizabeth.

It remained to be seen if Mary would become close to the widower whose sermon she found so enthralling and delightful that morning, as she described it in a letter she dispatched to him on Monday afternoon from Pemberley.

26.

On a day when the men had done a fine ride about the estate and eaten their midday meal on a terrace facing the west, the colonel ventured alone into the library. He was startled but not surprised to see that Catherine was sitting much as she so often had on Brook Street, immersed in a volume in a chair that had a grand view of the copse of trees to the north, beyond a pair of French doors.

She heard but ignored his entry until he was nearly upon her. She had long perfected the art of affectionate distance.

"Tell me, Colonel. What do you think of women?" she asked, without raising her head from the book she was reading.

"Is this from one of your novels?" he asked. "And has Mrs. Darcy proved to be someone whose taste in literature matches your own?"

She laughed at his manner of asking his question. "Oh, Colonel. I should not characterize this"—and she waved the volume—"as *literature*. It is nothing so presumptuous as that. It is merely a good tale. A novel."

He had moved to his own chair after collecting a volume for himself. "And what draws your attention so deeply?" she asked

"This?" He lifted his own volume to show her. "I should not presume to call it anything so dramatic as *literature* either. I promised myself that I would take steps to correct some of the deficiencies in my education now that I am concerned with where I am and where I am going more than where I have been."

"Oh, Colonel. Now you are sounding quite the philosopher."

He laughed as he replaced his book on his lap.

"It is perhaps that having been destined for a soldier's life, I suffered from a lack of learning of the things that my cousin enjoyed."

"Much, I daresay, as a woman is deprived. I do not know what Georgiana was taught but as for me and I believe my sisters Lizzy and Jane, we were long taught that our education began and ended with an ability to converse well in the company of men, to not be overbearing in the company of men. As to other characteristics of an accomplished lady, we scarcely had the most elemental teaching at best."

"I cannot speak for Georgiana," replied he, "but I believe her education did not differ greatly from that of any girl coming out in society."

"So, I imagine she and I are not so different in that respect."

He laughed. "I suppose not."

With that, they both quieted and as they had so often done on Brook Street and now at Pemberley, they fell into their separate yet somehow connected reads.

Some time later, he lifted his book and placed it on the table.

"The light is fading, Miss Bennet. My session here must come to an end. I would be pleased to accompany you wherever you are going. I believe I will enjoy your company as I go to my room to dress for dinner."

He stepped to her, trying to disguise his limp, which was futile and in her eyes something that had long since ceased to have any effect on her fondness for him. She placed her free arm through his, and together they awkwardly climbed to her room, where he left her so that he, too, could prepare for dinner.

Less than a week after the colonel arrived at Pemberley with the major, he asked Catherine whether if the morning's weather was favorable she could show him some of her preferred paths near the guest house.

And the weather was fine and they embarked on their tour.

Their movement sent their minds to work and after ten minutes or so she asked him for the first time about the war and its effect on him.

"It may well surprise you, Miss...Catherine, but as we rode slowly north after the battle, my thoughts were not about what should happen were I to die."

The notion visibly chilled her.

"Do not chastise me for so speaking. It is the reality about which no other words can suffice. But *that* was not my concern. To the contrary, I wondered often about would happen should I *live*. A soldier to be a soldier cannot fear death. Or think about it. It could happen at any moment in a battle. But we believe that dwelling on it only hastens the likelihood that it will occur."

She had never known someone, especially a man, to be so revealing of himself.

"No. As a soldier, I did not fear death, you see. Even afterwards, as we rode north and more and more of those who started the journey with me were removed for having died on the way, death was a constant companion but I did not allow it to become my obsession."

"I do not understand you, Richard."

"On that wagon in the Netherlands, I knew I would never fight again. That I would never again be a true soldier. Never again a leader of men. I would be a half blind, crippled civilian. Or worse. Hour upon hour on a rocky wagon lying. Until then, I could not have dared contemplate such a thing. So, for perhaps the first time, I was compelled to consider my life."

"And did you find a resolution?"

"I cannot say that I did. I can only say that I hope to someday have an answer."

These thoughts brought on a period of mutual silence. The two or three minute period was ended by Catherine.

"I think that I may well have run off with George Wickham if my younger sister had not gotten to him first and I might well have run off to Scotland with him I was so blinded...oh, Richard, I did not mean to be so insensitive."

She had never before confessed this.

"We are well past the point of thinking a stray remark, well meant, could pain me. I have more than enough other things to do so."

"I still am sorry. I meant that I had always been told that an officer was the type of man that a woman should aspire to having as a husband."

"An *officer* of the sort you would see marching and parading in his handsome regimentals and confident mien?"

"Of course. I knew that wars are not fought on parade grounds and that many, many die or are maimed. But the romance of a girl can be a powerful thing, particularly when her mother says again and again how she regretted not marrying an officer instead of the man she did marry."

Having met Mr. and Mrs. Bennet at the weddings and when they were in town for the great parade—*Wickham's parade*—the colonel felt lucky that Catherine had overcome those ill-conceived notions of an ideal husband.

"Now, having met you and traveled with you and all the rest," she resumed, "and no longer, I hope, being a girl, I have come to have some if slight understanding about the reality of war and its impact on those who fight them."

The colonel regretted that a girl's delusions had been adjusted by reality. Perhaps it would have been better that at least this one of Mrs. Bennet's daughters had retained the foolish notions of a soldier's life as Mrs. Bennet herself did, and as he thought Mrs. Wickham likely did as well.

There was no reason to mention that to the woman who had during their stroll through the Pemberley Woods moved inappropriately close to him but they were just emerging from the covered area and moving into sight of the great house and they separated themselves from the pleasantness of an intimacy neither had before known. Each asked the other what their plans were for the evening.

27

The colonel had not told anyone of the walk he had taken with Miss Bennet and did not know how he possibly could. It was far too intimate and remained uppermost in his mind. From that afternoon, he, and she, took advantage of every opportunity to take a turn on the grounds or to sit near one another in Pemberley's grand library.

To be sure, he had not fallen into the laziness of being a fool in love on a magnificent Derbyshire estate. He took advantage, too, of being an increasingly healthy man on the estate and even in the wet was seen riding its paths and trails, almost always with the major and as often as not, and more carefully, with Darcy and Bingley.

On one of these days, a Wednesday, when the four gentlemen took advantage of some fine weather to go for an extended ride, broken up by a fine meal at the Lambton Inn while their horses were cared for, spirits were quite high when they surrendered their mounts to a pair of Pemberley grooms and went in.

As soon as they were through the front door, the butler stepped up to the colonel and said that a footman from Haverford House was awaiting him in the sitting room.

"I believe he has a letter for you, sir," the butler said as he went to open the room's door. Upon entering, the footman stood stiffly, having heard the foursome's approach on the drive.

"Beggin' your pardon, sir." He bowed, and the colonel saw the letter in the man's right hand. "I been instructed to deliver this to you in person, sir."

He lifted the envelope, still not having moved, and the colonel stepped up to him and relieved him of it. He recognized his father's hand, an intricate scrolled "Richard Fitzwilliam, Col. (ret.)"

"Thank you, Gilles. You may go now," the colonel said, "but do not leave yet until I have seen what my father has said."

The servant bowed and stepped into the foyer, closing the door behind himself and telling the butler that he had been instructed to wait for instructions. The two stood together.

In the meantime, the colonel ripped the seal apart to get at the contents. His father had never written to him like this before, a message delivered by a footman.

The stationery was heavy but it was not the formal sort generally used by the earl. There was no imprinting on it.

Richard,

I beg that you come to the house forthwith. A matter of extreme importance has been brought to my attention. Be assured that it has nothing to do with the health of your mother or of anyone else in the household. I dare not provide the details in this letter but only request that you accompany Gilles back at your earliest convenience.

Father

The colonel was at a complete loss for what this could mean but there was no question that he must go with the footman.

Darcy and the major were dawdling in the foyer waiting for the colonel to tell them what was important enough for his father to send someone to collect him.

"I cannot say what it is," he told them. "I do not know myself. It is a cryptic message instructing me to go to Haverford House with all deliberate speed. I am sorry,

Darcy. But I must beg to be allowed to ride the horses you have so generously left at my disposal here."

"What about me?" the major asked. "I will accompany you." He turned to Darcy. "I trust I may ride the mare assigned to me?"

Darcy waved his arms for calm.

"You shall both be accommodated, I assure you." To the butler he said, "Please have Cook prepare something that they can take on the trip. Also for the footman, if you please."

The butler bowed and was gone to the kitchen.

"While that is being seen to, get yourself ready. If you do not dither, you should have light until you reach the house. You, of course, will take your horses. I only ask that you send a message to me the moment you have learned what is so urgent that you must leave here so precipitously and to tell me what your plans are."

28

The three men rode hard but not recklessly. They stopped several times at stables along the way to give their mounts a chance to recover and arrived at Haverford House just as the day was drifting away. A groom came to them in front of the house and he took the Pemberley horses to be cooled down with the footman joining him with his own, exhausted Haverford stallion.

The front door opened before they reached it. Though they were hardly fit to be seen from their ride, the colonel was told that his father and mother were waiting for him in the former's study on the first floor. A footman accompanied the major to his familiar room so he, at least, could recover.

Lord and Lady Waddington had seen the men approach. They stood when their son entered the room.

"I am sorry to require that you come on such short notice and without giving you the opportunity to make yourself presentable," the earl said, "but this is a matter of upmost importance."

The colonel gave his mother a kiss on the cheek and the three sat down. The colonel was opposite his parents in the room's ornate armchairs.

"Yes, Father."

The earl coughed. The countess diverted her eyes down.

"It is most unpleasant so I will get straight to it. Did you know an Estelle Maines?"

A flood washed over the colonel.

"Did I?"

"She is dead, son."

The colonel could not have anticipated this. He could understand being exposed. But *dead*?

"I do not understand. I know of this Estelle Maines." He paused and understood it was no time to be evasive. He leaned forward, a movement that got his mother's attention and set her eyes to look up at him.

"Might I be correct, Father, in saying that you have been made aware of a liaison that I had with that woman some ten years ago? And that the product of that passing intimacy is a boy who is about ten today?"

"You are correct, sir. I have been made aware of this. That you lay with an unmarried farm girl on the estate and put her in the family way. That she married before she gave birth, to a farmer unaware of what you had done to his bride. That he raised the child as his own, as he reasonably thought he was. And you did nothing for the boy."

"That is all true, Father. But—"

"No *buts*, son. I have been made aware of all of these facts and you do not deny them."

"I do not."

"Then you must take responsibility for what has recently occurred."

"I will take responsibility. I hope you understand that about me."

"Yet you do not know of what I speak." The earl's voice was tightening and his wife took in a deep breath.

"You will not know that she, this...whore is dead. Killed brutally by her husband when he discovered that he had been lied to for years and years."

"Murdered?" The colonel lost several shades in the shock. "Murdered? But she did nothing wrong."

The earl was in full fire, leaning towards his second son, his hands gripping the intricately carved wooden arms of his patterned chair, his knuckles whitening.

"Of course she did something wrong. I do not acquit you in the slightest for your immoral conduct with her, a woman under the protection of the estate. Do what you will with the whores in London or in trains following the Army but how dare you take advantage of a woman on one of our farms soon to marry one of our tenant farmers!"

The colonel had never seen the anger viciously being displayed in front of him. Even his mother's slight attempt at calming the earl with her hand was fruitless. He simply pulled his hand violently from her grip.

"I will not have it, sir. I will not have it."

"I am sorry, Father. Mother. It was an indiscretion. I only learned recently that a son was the product of our brief moment of connection."

"*Connection* you say! You have not heard the worst of it. The husband, the man you abused so horribly, the man you knew she was betrothed to when you lay with her has hanged himself. In the barn of the farm he rented *from me*. I cannot say how he discovered what she had done, but however it was, he could not tolerate that knowledge. He killed her and like a coward he killed himself."

These images were flashing through the colonel's mind.

"What about the boy?"

"Your son? He at least was spared by this madness for which you are responsible. What's to become of him we cannot say."

His mother spoke at last. "I would do what I could for him as he is my grandchild. But your father says that that would be most inappropriate."

"Of course it would," the earl said. "And I cannot imagine anyone would allow it."

"Does he have any family?" the colonel asked.

"I cannot say, son. I have been told that at least for now he is being cared for. What will happen when the sin of his birth overcomes the town's immediate grief, I cannot say."

"We will," the Countess said, "do whatever we can for him, even if we have no other contact. We will provide for him as necessary."

"Which was my intent when I learned of him," the colonel said. "But I did not know what could be done without upsetting the happy life that Estelle said she had established with her husband."

"Until he found out the truth," his father said dismissively. "How could you have been such a fool? With one of our own girls? And how will your mother and I be able to show our faces again in Waddington? How?"

The colonel looked at his mother and realized the extent of the damage. He stood and went to the window in the room's sudden silence. He looked out over the grounds he had loved for so long, that he missed in those days and months in the Peninsula and on the Continent just over the past year. *Will I ever enjoy this view again?* he asked himself.

He took a deep breath and turned, his form silhouetted against the reddish sunset.

"What am I to do?"

His parents looked at one another.

"Son," his father said, "I am afraid for at least some time you must be in exile. Perhaps it will not be for long but these are not Londoners. These are Lincolnshire folk. They are *our* folk. Go to town. You will never be content here, now that you have gone through the world as you have gone through it. Stay with your brother as you determine what you can make of yourself."

He stood and closed the gap with his second son. He put his arm on his shoulder.

"I know you are a good man. I know what you did was in fact something natural for a virile man like yourself and that but for the child it would not have mattered except to this Estelle and her husband, if she ever confessed to him what she had done. But fate, as you well know from the field of battle, can be cruel and arbitrary."

The colonel thought of all the good men who had been cut down, from General Ponsonby killed by those French lancers to the country privates shattered by French artillery. His penance, whatever it was, paled in comparison.

"Richard," his mother said across to him. "You will always be foremost in our hearts and thoughts but I agree with your father that you must find a different way for yourself."

"I assume," his father said, "that you have been wrestling with that since the morning after the great battle where you suffered so grievously."

"Not nearly so much as others suffered."

"Posh. Put that aside. We are speaking about you. All I can advise is that you go to town, perhaps with the major, and do what you can do to redeem yourself, not least in your own mind."

29.

After leaving his parents, the colonel went to the major's room. The guest was sitting in a chair by his window reading but was on his feet as soon as he heard the knock.

The colonel told him of the tragedy that his indiscretion a decade before had led to. He said he would be leaving the next morning for London to ease the strain on his parents and the estate.

"I leave it to you, Major, to decide whether to go with me to my uncertain fate. I realize that you have developed certain feelings for my cousin and I will not deny you the opportunity to return to her at Pemberley to see if you can bring them to fruition."

The major shook his head.

"That was all likely just a passing fancy on my part, sir. It hardly matters. I do not know where you are going or are thinking of going but I did not accompany you this far only to be abandoned in your time of need."

"Groeper," said the colonel, looking at his underling. "This is my battle and mine alone. I will not deprive you of the future you have been so looking forward to once you had fulfilled your duties as to me. I assure you that you have done that and more and I release you from any further obligations to me."

"With all due respect, sir," Groeper said, his feet firmly spaced and his anger mounting, "I have not been with you all this time and over all this distance, sir, to be dismissed as not being needed when I so plainly am. Do not insult us both by pretending otherwise. I will not abandon you. Sir."

"I cannot ask you to come along, Michael. But I will not deny you if that is your firm intention."

"It is."

"Then we must make it so. My father has allowed me to take one of his carriages to Lincoln in the morning. From there we will take the post to London."

"I agree, sir. Do you have any money? I have some, but I do not know if it will be enough for two tickets to London."

The colonel reached into a pocket in his satchel. He withdrew a number of bills.

"I have enough for us to at least sit inside and have decent enough food and drink along the way."

"Along the way where, sir?"

"I will go to my brother's first. My father said he sent his own letter, but I must tell him myself that I, now *we* it appears, are coming to London. I will send him an express. We will not remain there, though. I hope he can provide some money for us until we settle on what we are to do. We can stay at the Regimental Club."

"I perhaps will stay with my parents, sir, if that would be acceptable to you."

"Anything you elect to do will be acceptable to me."

He restored the bills to his satchel.

"Now you must see to your things," he said.

They spent an uneasy night after dining together in the colonel's room. His father did not come to him but his mother did very late.

He was pleased if surprised when he had responded to her knocking softly on his door and seen her in the hall. He insisted that she sit in one of the pair of armchairs in the room and he took its twin.

After composing herself with a deep breath, she said, "Richard, I cannot imagine what you are going through. Perhaps it is more than you went through on that muddy field you so hate to speak of. I cannot say. I forgive you for what happened here and I know that your father will, in time."

He found his eyes beginning to water and fought to keep his mother from seeing it. She was steely, displaying a countess's practiced and hard-won control.

"I promise you your son's situation will be utmost in our thoughts and prayers. I have spoken to your father and he agrees he is in part our responsibility even if he is right that we can only do what is appropriate. But whatever that is, we shall do."

Her son could no longer keep his emotions concealed and he blubbered his thanks, saying, "I do not know where I am but I will do whatever is required of me."

"I know, son, I know," she said, reaching across the gap between them to grasp his hands, hands so much larger than her own.

She stood and he did as well.

"There is one more thing your father has asked me to convey to you. When you arrive in town, he will have arranged for a generous amount to be made available to you at his bank. You know it. It will, we hope, suffice to keep you together, body and soul, until you set out to do what it is you set out to do."

"Thank you, mother," the colonel said, as he wrapped his arms around her and pulled her close in a manner he had never done before and that he was certain he would likely never do again.

They separated, now both having given in to the force of what they were feeling for one another, and he opened the door for her to leave. Which she did, after he gave her a final, "Thank you, mother."

30

In the morning, five dispatches left Haverford House. Three were for Pemberley. Two were going to London.

The former consisted of a letter from the colonel to Mr. and Mrs. Fitzwilliam Darcy, one from him to Miss Catherine Bennet, and one from Major Groeper to Georgiana Darcy.

Going to the south were a letter from the colonel to his brother and a letter from the major to his own parents in Cheapside.

The letters were of varying degrees of intimacy. Those sent west revealed the essential news concerning what had happened to Estelle Maines and her husband. There was little news at least at Haverford House concerning the son, the colonel's acknowledged son, and all that could be said about that was that he had been taken into the care of someone and that now that his lineage had been revealed the family had offered to do whatever it could to support its newest, albeit half-, member.

The letters to London were more formal, doing little more than informing the respective recipients of the impending arrival under exigent circumstances of the relevant family member.

Not long after those letters were gone, the two officers said their goodbyes to Lord and Lady Waddington and boarded the finest of the family's carriages with the major's scant belongings added to the colonel's in a trunk for the short trip to Lincoln. Each had a solid breakfast while the trunk was lashed to the brougham's rear.

Before the carriage began its trip, Lord Waddington stepped to it. He looked in, with his wife nearby.

"Son, Major. I am sorry that matters have come to this. We need not speak more of it. I, and your mother, son, wish the both of you God speed and a clear road ahead. We hope you will be able to return here but we know that you, both of you, will remain in our thoughts wherever you find yourselves to be."

With that, he looked up at the coachman and gave him a definitive *Drive on* and soon the brougham disappeared in the dust on the drive that led to Waddington and then to Lincoln.

They could have bypassed the town but elected not to. They suffered the silence of those they passed, so at odds with the huzzahs that had greeted them. They could do nothing but give furtive glances at what they passed and each wondered, too, whether they would ever be in the village again but each understood that they probably never would. They were leaving.

31

The two officers were well south of Lincoln when their letters reached Pemberley. Their recipients had been waiting in uncertainty after the colonel's sudden summons to Haverford House and all manner of speculations were bounding about the estate, including among the servants, who had no better idea than did anyone else.

Darcy stepped out to the drive when the rider with the letters appeared. He paid for them and was quickly joined by the others. Catherine and Georgiana went quickly to their rooms with the words from their gentlemen and Darcy and Elizabeth were left alone in the relative intimacy of her study with theirs.

My Dear Friends,

I was called to my parents to address the consequences of an action I took some ten years ago. I will not delve deeply into the matter beyond saying that I lay with a soon to be married woman on one of the estate's farms and she bore a child from our congress. A boy. I learned of the child's existence only recently, before I left for the continent, when the mother told me. She said her husband understood the child to be his and that there was no reason to alter the equilibrium that she and her husband, a farmer on another of the estate's farms, had established with the boy.

For reasons I do not understand, the husband became aware of the lineage of the boy recently. He reacted in a most barbaric manner. He killed his wife and then hanged himself. The boy, thank God, was left unharmed. I understand that he has been taken in by relatives in Waddington.

I have shattered, perhaps irrevocably, the honor of my family. At the least, I must remove myself as far as possible. The major has agreed to accompany me to London. Whether we will remain there, I cannot say. I will advise you of my intentions when I arrive at them.

I most ardently wish that my conduct not create any more of a taint on our family than is necessary. So I will distance myself from the family at least for the short term.

Because my situation will become generally known shortly, feel free to disclose the contents of this letter to the Bingleys. Miss Catherine and Georgiana will be made aware of it in the letters being sent to them separately.

Richard

The letters to the two women were similar in tone and they would be shared, but only between them. Each told in general terms the calamity that had taken place in Waddington and of the necessity that the colonel leave. Each letter did its best to be the sort of final letter often made by a military man, that he be forgotten and that she find someone more worthy of her love. That she will never be forgotten and he will never be worthy of a good woman's love.

And on the post heading south, just reaching the outskirts of Peterborough, the authors of those letters were themselves hoping with scant confidence that they might be able to forget the women they loved.

32

The colonel expected that there would be much turmoil at Pemberley when the letters arrived. It could not be helped. He was glad for the level heads of both his cousin and of Elizabeth. He was deeply troubled, though, about Catherine. He had long admired her and he enjoyed his time with her more than he could say. It was a gradual thing, growing with each of their encounters in Darcy's library in town and in the one in the country. In the walks they took. Even when they were with others they somehow managed to drift slightly apart from the Darcys and the Bingleys they had started out with.

Surely Elizabeth at least noticed. Darcy, even as softened by his wife, perhaps had too much of the masculine blindness for the amorous.

The colonel and the major had been able to get seats inside on the first of the day's post carriages out of Lincoln. The weather was adequate through the first day, miserable the second, and very fine on the third. They were largely silent throughout the ride, each in his own world, dealing politely with the inevitable inquiries about whether they had been in the army and whether they had fought in the great battle and whether, the bolder of those with them asked, the injury to the older of the two was a result of being in that battle.

As it was clear that neither former officer wished to dwell, they were largely left alone with their thoughts, and to ignore the stares that flooded their way when they left the carriage while the horses were being changed or when they ate at an inn for the night.

They reached the station near the Thames not far from Parliament and were glad to be free of the small space and the companions with whom they shared it.

They took their satchels and got aboard a cab that took the pair to the colonel's brother's house in Mayfair.

33

"Lizzy, I will get to him whether you help me or not." Catherine was with her sister. It was early on the morning after they had received the letters from the colonel, when the two officers were about to set off on the second day of their journey.

Catherine had found Lizzy sitting at her small table with its looking glass, running a brush through her hair. Neither of them had slept well or much. Catherine was sitting on Lizzy's bed and Lizzy remained on her bench but turned.

"Stop being a child. He is gone. He is not coming back. You must look elsewhere for your future. It is not with him. It cannot be with him."

Catherine's anger nearly burst. She was not being a child. She was being a woman. For perhaps the first time in her life she was being a woman. And as a woman, she would not abandon Richard. She did not care what he had done. The man had nearly been killed at Waterloo and survived and she *knew* he would survive this, and she *knew* she must be with him when he did and perhaps to help him as he did.

He had not admitted it, but she knew that he had come to love her. She could not say why or how. But of all the things of the world, this was perhaps the one about which she had the least doubt. That and her love for him, revealed definitively in recent days.

"Will you help me get to him?"

"You do not even know where he is. He could be anywhere. He might not even be heading to London. And even if he is, how will you find him?"

"I will find him," Catherine made clear. "I do not know how, but I will. I will go to his brother's. I will go to his

Regimental Club. I will go to the War Office. I will find him."

Lizzy stood and reached for Catherine's hand and directed her to sit with her on the bed.

"I know you wish to be supportive of him—"

"I love him, Lizzy. You know that."

"I do and I am glad you are at last ready to announce it. You are right in thinking that he loves you. I am sure of that, though he's not spoken a word of that to me or, so far as I know, to Darcy. But the reality is that you will be ruined and perhaps I'm afraid will ruin us were you to attach himself to him."

Catherine began to rise, but Lizzy put her hand on her sister's thigh to make her remain.

"So this is about you?" Catherine said violently.

Lizzy understood that it was not an unreasonable accusation and she herself wondered how much of it was the truth. She had worked hard to elevate the Bennets to become part of a distinguished family. Even Lydia's hurried marriage to Wickham had not prevented Elizabeth Darcy from becoming one of the first ladies of Derbyshire and for invitations to their house in London to become much sought after.

Yes, the Bennets had survived Lydia's infamous marriage, but this could be too much. Elizabeth had responsibilities beyond the Bennets. To the Darcys. To her Fitzwilliam. To Georgiana.

Elizabeth rose. No. Catherine was acting in just the childish manner as Lydia had, being besotted by an officer, throwing all care and caution and decorum to the wind for, in this case, a forever tarnished man. She would not help her sister, love be damned. Great love even. She had read those novels, too. She sometimes thought she had practically lived in one, though it would be a very poor novelist who would think that anyone would have an interest in her simple life.

"I am sorry. It is out of the question. You will stay here. You will forget him—"

"Forget him?"

"You *must* forget him. You know you must. He has fled. Of his own volition he has fled. He has left you. I am sure that in doing so he understood that his love for you was strong enough that he would give you up so that you would not be destroyed in having any connection to him."

She turned back to Catherine, who had not moved from where she sat on the bed.

"That is it, my dear sister. He has done it in part because he *does* love you, and you must treasure that ray of hope. You must treat him as a man who gave himself up for others. For you. Grieve and mourn. But you will stay with Darcy and me. We will return to town, and you will be presented, and you will always have a memory with him, but you must have a family with another."

Catherine could tolerate this condescension no more. She was up and quickly around Elizabeth and through the door she opened. Lizzy let her go.

As Catherine headed to her room, Elizabeth put a robe on and walked to her husband's bedchamber. She knocked, but there was no answer and a footman in the hall told her that he was already up and had gone down for his breakfast. It was unusual, but she did not bother to get into a dress and instead headed down to the dining parlor, where she found her husband staring out to the Pemberley Woods with a cup of coffee in his hand.

He turned when he heard the interruption. He dismissed the footman on duty in the room as his wife stepped up to him.

"We must speak of Catherine," she said.

"I know. It is very messy, I'm afraid. He does love her, you know."

"Yes, they love each other. And now he is gone."

After saying this, Elizabeth stepped up to her husband. "And she wishes to follow him." He put his cup down to the saucer in his left hand and placed them on the windowsill. "It is quite impossible," he said.

"That is what I told her. I do not think I convinced her."

"Give her some time. She will come to her senses."

She turned to him, running her hand down his arm.

"That's just it, Fitzwilliam. I do not know that she should."

This jarred him. "What do you mean?"

"Can we sit?" They both realized she was in her gown with a robe over it and a pair of slippers on her feet. He led her across the foyer to the sitting room, where they could have privacy with the door closed. When they both sat, she said, "She told me that our unwillingness to help her—"

"To help her in a most inappropriate venture."

"Fitzwilliam, please. Allow me to finish my thought. She accused me of thinking not of her and her feelings towards your cousin or his toward her but of the Darcy name and reputation."

"What is wrong with that? They have both been beneficiaries of the Darcy name and fortune. It is hardly appropriate that she attack it."

"I agree that the name must be protected. But there must be something that we can do."

The pair heard the front door of the house open, though it was still very early. They were close enough to the window to the east to see Catherine striding down towards the lake, through the mist of the morning dew. She was not carrying anything with her. She was going for a walk, not planning to flee to Lambton and from there to London.

"She is miserable," Elizabeth said.

"She will survive this disappointment. Richard is gone and gone forever. She will come back to town with us after the season and we will resume our lives and she will find her husband."

"It is as if he died in battle. That's what you are saying?"

There was something in her tone that disturbed him, but the reality was that that was exactly what it was like. He was dead to the proper world. There would be no burial. No services at which he would be remembered and events in his life would be recalled. Dead. That is how it must be, and that is how Catherine must view it.

"She will never do it," Elizabeth said.

"She is just a child. She has no choice."

"Fitzwilliam. She is more like me than any of my other sisters and you know how stubborn I was. And am."

He did know that. Catherine was just entering the path that led to the lake, and they resumed their seats.

"I married you for love," she said. "And I would have married you were you a pauper. I truly believe I would have. And I truly believe that Catherine wishes to marry your cousin even if they never have a proper home and have a lonely existence with just the two of them and such off-spring as they may be blessed with."

Darcy always enjoyed Elizabeth's description of her true desire for him as a man though he felt himself inadequate to professing the similar affection he had for her. Putting Catherine in her position made Darcy less certain in his initial assessment. *Could anything be done without destroying the family, and especially Georgiana and any little Darcys as he and Elizabeth might produce together?*

Darcy abruptly jumped to his feet.

"We must allow it."

"It?" she asked.

"Were he a stranger, we would bar the doors. But he is my cousin. He is a good man, as you know he is."

She nodded. "Notwithstanding his foolishness."

"A young man's, young soldier's, foolishness."

*   *   *   *

Not ten minutes after Elizabeth learned that Catherine had returned from her walk, Elizabeth rapped lightly on her sister's door. Without waiting, she opened it and saw her sister lying on her back on her bed

"Darcy and I have spoken of your situation. You will be happy to know that he agrees with you more perhaps than he agrees with me."

"I may go?"

Elizabeth sat on the side of the bed.

"Yes, my dear. You may go. I will write to our uncle Gardiner and you will go to him. As you know from what happened with Lydia, he is quite adept at difficult situations and I trust him to being able to help you."

With some awkwardness, Catherine managed to get up and in front of her sister to hug her as tears escaped from her.

"Thank you, Lizzy. I know it will be alright."

"We will have one of our footmen accompany you and you will write to me at least twice a week. Is that understood?"

"Perfectly."

"Good. Now we will arrange for you to go to London. Is that acceptable?"

"More than. Thank you."

34.

In her room next to Catherine's, Georgiana had heard the animated voices of her friend and her sister-in-law, rising and falling during the course of the conversation. Finally, after things between those two had calmed, she heard the door open and close.

After waiting several more minutes and hearing nothing, Georgiana herself went to Catherine's room. After a light knock that seemed to echo though the quiet hallway, she was told to come in.

"What is your plan?" she asked after taking several strides into the room and seeing her friend sitting at her bureau.

"Plan?"

"Do not treat me for a fool, Catherine. You intend to follow my cousin do you not?" She sat on the side of the bed and Catherine turned on her bench to face her.

"I cannot *not* follow him," she said, keeping her eyes on the other but rolling her hands against one another.

Georgiana rose and squatted awkwardly beside her, her plain cream house dress limiting her movement. She reached over to wrap an arm around.

"Of course I know that." She gave her friend a tap. "And," still at a whisper, "you must know that I must follow my own soldier."

Catherine felt something course through her and recovered her senses enough to turn sharply.

"Michael? No, Georgie, you would be throwing yourself away."

"And you are not?"

They held each other's eyes.

"We both know that they are connected. And that we are thus connected. And we have no choice but to go to the ends of the earth with them."

She reached into her bosom and removed the letter that she had received when Catherine had received the colonel's. She kissed it and handed it to Catherine.

"I have read it a thousand times," she said. "It is as clear to me as Richard's was to you. Read it again."

My Dearest,

You must forget me. I was forced to the hardest and harshest decision a man can be put to, but I must put duty and honor before love. I fear you will be tainted and that is something that is not tolerable for me.

I pray that you find a man who is deserving of your love and affection, as I never was, and I fear never will be.

Yours,
M

Catherine looked up when she finished and handed it back to her friend. It was quickly restored to the place of intimacy where Catherine understood it perhaps would always be kept at least in spirit. Even in the low light, she could see tears forming in Georgiana's eyes.

And she was right, was Georgiana. Catherine had received the same sentiments from her lover.

Georgiana stood and returned to the bed as Catherine straightened up on her little bench, all of the immediate emotional having been put aside.

"Now you must tell me your plan."

*   *   *   *

When that discussion ended, the two found Elizabeth in her study and asked her if she could send for Darcy, which Lizzy sent a footman to see to.

Before he arrived, Elizabeth confirmed that the two had discussed Catherine's plans and that she and Darcy had agreed to support her and that Georgiana had taken it upon herself to join. Receiving confirmation, she said they needed to wait until he arrived.

When he did it in a bit of a huff, the three were seated in patterned armchairs, and he took the fourth, forming something of a circle.

Elizabeth reached for her husband's hand.

"Your sister has something to ask of you."

He was hardly surprised. He and Elizabeth had spoken about it at length after approval for Catherine's departure had been extended.

Georgiana cleared her throat and attempted to speak but found her brother's stare, however kindly he meant it to be, intimidating but only for a moment. If she was to pursue her affection, she could not be irresolute and ended the awkwardness with a statement, unadorned and unflinching, that she would be going with Catherine.

Taken aback by her vehemence but also somehow pleased by it, Darcy had conceded to himself and to Elizabeth that his sister was, as was Catherine, a woman with her own mind who he could not, and should not, be kept in however gilded a cage he might make for her. Her experience with Wickham was a lifetime ago and that naïve girl was no more.

And he truly respected Major Groeper. He had proven himself in countless ways to his cousin and while, as the colonel had anticipated, that his eyes might be more on Georgiana's fortune than they were on Georgiana herself had occurred to him, he had measured his conduct and his words very carefully and had satisfied himself that it was appropriate that he pass her protection to this good, brave man. Whose bravery was again established by his immediate willingness to, as it were, once more go into the breach with the colonel.

To Georgiana, her brother's quick willingness to allow her to go on her journey came as a surprise but it was in fact the end and logical result of his having given much thought to this question. And when he said he would support her, and Catherine and the two officers, in any way he could, she leapt from her chair and threw herself at him and wrapped her arms around him to such a degree that he, and Elizabeth, for a moment feared that he would be strangled in the enthusiasm. In the end, though, all was made right and making the vague plans of seeking out the colonel and the major into reality became their next task.

35.

Before they went in for dinner, Darcy made an announcement to his guests. Jane, Bingley, and Mary were largely put to the side as the plans were set in place. They had been told of the general situation that had led the colonel to leave Pemberley and that he and the major were *en route* to London to an uncertain fate. To this he added that he and Elizabeth had agreed to support Catherine and Georgiana in their decision to go to the two officers.

These others had more immediate and personal matters to attend to, with Jane still healthy and Mary still tending to her and Bingley preoccupied and exchanging letters with his sisters about Jane's condition and the baby's prospects. They understood, though, why the two women needed to travel to town.

By nightfall, Catherine and Georgiana had packed their trunks. They would take a Pemberley brougham to town. Two footmen would accompany them and then join the slight crew of servants at the Darcy house on Brook Street in case they were needed.

The women would be staying with the Gardiners. Better than to being alone on Brook Street. Elizabeth had written to her aunt and uncle explaining the situation and asking that they provide whatever assistance they could to Catherine and Georgiana in their quest.

Everyone in the household had come down for breakfast and when that was over and Catherine and Georgiana had time for their final preparations, they were all on the Pemberley drive, where the carriage awaited them.

Farewells were said all about and promises were made of frequent communications and soon the carriage with its two occupants and their trunks rolled away toward Lambton and from there continuing up to London.

36

Catherine and Georgiana were still in the early part of their own journey when Colonel Fitzwilliam and Major Groeper reached town and had appeared at Lord Ashworth's. At the house's door, they rang and were promptly admitted by the butler who knew them from their earlier visits. They waited in the foyer for just a moment as Lord and Lady Ashworth were soon down to greet them.

The four went into the sitting room. The colonel's note had only been received early the prior evening and their father's earlier that day. The colonel insisted that they would not impose and that he would be staying at his Regimental Club while the major would be either there or at his parents' small house in Cheapside. That explained and refreshments having been brought in, and the officers rejecting Lord Ashworth's suggesting that they at least each have a bath to recover from their journey, Lady Ashworth excused herself to allow the gentlemen to converse in comfort.

The major soon left as well, insisting that it would be best that he go to his parents' to make himself presentable and promising to return for dinner. He had sent his own note to them before leaving Haverford House.

Lord Ashworth suggested he and his brother adjourn to the greater intimacy of his library. It was a cluttered, stuffy place, filled with all manner of manuscripts and documents laying haphazardly around. On the walls were shelf after shelf of tomes, and several stuffed animal specimens were enclosed in glass on a long table near the room's sole window.

John's desk itself was covered in papers scattered about as were the two chairs that were set opposite his own, dark leather one. But a place was made for his brother and the two sat across the large desk.

"I will get straight to it. I have been the engine of a horror and the death of an innocent woman."

John rose and stepped to a table behind the desk on which there was an assortment of Irish crystal decanters containing various beverages as well as glasses of varying sizes. While his brother watched him, John unstopped one containing a fine Scottish whisky and poured some in a pair of broad glasses.

Without a word, he brought one to the colonel and then resumed his own seat.

"I think you may need this." His brother thanked him and took a long sip and felt it hurry through him and acted as a calming elixir.

"Our father was very circumspect."

"What did he say?"

"Only that you had been accused of an...indiscretion from some years ago and that it recently resulted in a tragedy. That is the death of innocents. He said he intended to make his revulsion clear to you—"

"I assure you that he did, which explains my presence here."

"Indeed. He also said at least for now you are not welcome at Haverford Hall."

He took a deep sigh and leaned back.

"That, too," the colonel said softly, "is true."

His brother leaned forward, still cradling his glass in his hands.

"Now, Rich, tell me what it is you wish to tell me."

The colonel never appreciated his brother's scientific mind as he did at that moment. John understood and would listen dispassionately to what needed to be said and would give his dispassionate advice.

Holding his own glass in his lap between his palms, he told of his encounter with Estelle Maines and the product of that liaison. How he had only learned of it when he was about to leave for the final battle with Bonaparte. How the husband, Howard Maines, never knew and had fully accepted the boy as his own, natural son. The shocking news that swept through Waddington and the ensuing deaths of both himself—by his own hand—and his wife. At her husband's hand.

"There's not much else I can say, John," the colonel ended, his shoulders dropping and his voice low. "As soon as I learned of what I had done, what I had caused, I had to leave Lincolnshire as father says and here I am. I hope when word reaches town that *you* will not be destroyed by it. I could not remain anywhere near Haverford Hall. Our parents have been hurt far too much already by my sin."

He did not realize that in his speaking, he had returned to the glass several times so it was empty. Without a word, his brother rose from his chair. He lifted the decanter and carried it to his brother, who held up his glass to be refilled. This was done and after restoring the decanter whence it came, John returned to his seat.

"This is a bad business, Rich. I know it is. It cannot help but badly affect you and me and our parents. We must be resigned to that, though fortunately none of us is as exposed to the gossip and disapproval of strangers, our parents' preferred isolation being a blessing in this case, as is my own non-conformist views of my position."

Lord Ashworth stood and moved some papers on a credenza to reveal a cigar box. He offered one to his brother, who took and lit it. The colonel then took a long draw as his brother resumed his seat.

"Now," said his lordship, "what are your thoughts about what's to be done with you?"

Both Richard and Major Groeper had, of course, given this question much consideration.

"Whatever I do," the colonel said, "it must not soil our family's name or that of my cousin."

"Darcy?"

"Yes, Darcy. He and his family have been too kind to me, and I will not burden that kindness."

"I fully agree. What are your options? What can you...*do*?"

Lord Ashworth took another draw on his cigar, and his visitor did the same as the dank odor began to fill the room, there being no fresh air with the window closed.

There was little more to do at this point, and John rose. His brother did too.

"You will stay for dinner, of course."

"Thank you. I will."

Before they left the study, Lord Ashworth again asked his brother, "And, again, Rich. What of you?"

"Perhaps I shall go to America."

"America? Do you mean to flee us entirely?"

"Do I have a choice? I am best forgotten by going to New York or some such place far from these shores. I'm sure I can find something to keep body and so much of my soul as I still possess together. Indeed, probably far easier than I can anywhere in England."

"You have thought on this? Are you going to the wilderness of the Ohio Valley? That would be absurd."

The colonel shook his head. "Nothing so ambitious as that. I do have my one good eye, of course, but I think it best if I keep it in a more...civilized world."

"If one can be found anywhere on those shores. Why not Canada?"

The colonel again rejected the idea.

"I had much time to think on this as I came to London. It will be best to explore New York. I think I can get some introductions through one of Father's banks in that city. I will include a request about that in what I send to him later. But it should be enough for someone like me.'

He took a long final drag on his cigar and put it out in a plate on the desk.

"Many soldiers sent there have elected to remain with their American brides. Those in America will not, I should imagine, care a farthing for our little scandal. They are all about money, and perhaps I can make some there and forget about or at least move on from this whole sordid business here."

"Perhaps, you can, Rich. Perhaps you can."

He slapped his brother on the shoulder as they entered the hall.

"Shall we tell Isobel?" Lord Ashworth asked. "I think we must."

"We must," and so the two men left the cluttered study and headed to the sitting room with John instructing a footman to ask his wife to join them. When she did, Richard repeated in broad strokes the tale of how he came to cause, or at the least bear responsibility for, the deaths in Waddington, and Isobel joined her husband in agreeing that they would do what they could to ensure that the colonel could have a life, even if it was in America.

37

The clear blue sky with only a splattering of clouds proved short-lived for Catherine and Georgiana on their own trip south. About two hours after they were gone from Pemberley and well south of Sheffield, the carriage was driving into darker and darker clouds. Within three, the rain was pelting it and the coachman and footmen and horses mercilessly.

As for the women inside, umbrellas could do only so much so when they were forced to leave the carriage to take care of necessities when the horses were changed, they returned damp for their efforts. Thus did the first day pass, mercifully ended as they rolled into Leicester and stopped before an old inn. Their trunks were carried in and they were able to bathe and change into dry clothes.

Finally, when they were in their room and dinner was brought to them, they were able to review the day's affairs but for only so long as their exhaustion got the better of them and both fell into deep sleeps the moment their bodies were in their bed.

The weather changed overnight, so the second and third days of their journey passed pleasantly enough. They repeated their recoveries at an inn in Luton the second night, this time dining in the tavern under the watchful eyes of their servants sitting nearby trying to be as inconspicuous as possible.

In a quiet moment on the morning of the third day, Catherine asked Georgiana about Major Groeper.

"I do not quite understand your attachment," said Miss Bennet.

Georgiana put her hand beneath the other's arm and leaned closer, the better to be unheard by the others.

"It came on slowly, as I believe was the case with your Colonel."

"Yes, that is true."

"And like what I witnessed with the two of you, it began in the most innocent of ways. You know my great love for the pianoforte, which my brother has encouraged me in and I admit spoiled me in. While Michael of course heard me when I played to the group, he wandered into the drawing room one afternoon while I was playing. He tried to be coy at first and then got up the courage to ask me if he could assist me in my playing by turning the pages of my scores, which I, of course, allowed him to do.

"After several times, I began to anticipate his stumbling upon me. Mind you, I should not have liked or even tolerated anyone else doing so."

"Even your brother?"

"Especially my brother. Though I admit to having something of a soft spot for your sister and would have allowed her to remain, though she never did. Especially after I think she realized that Michael was *assisting me* with my playing. By then I was very glad when he entered and sat beside me on the bench to turn the pages."

"He was on your bench?" Catherine asked. "Did he...touch you?"

"The bench was not very wide so that was inevitable and I may have been very wrong in this but I sometimes scooted over so that my leg would be touching his. And I will say as fine and proper an officer as he was, he never did separate his from mine."

"Thank God you brother was not there."

"Especially since I intentionally selected pieces where a page turn was necessary. *Do you sing?* I asked him at one point and when he said he did not sing well but enjoyed it I placed a Mozart song I had collected for this purpose on the music stand and he sang while I played.

"Before he had finished the first rondo, I knew an affection had grown in me for him."

Catherine found herself drifting to those long ago days at the Darcys' house in London when she had happened by the music room and hear Georgiana's fine voice and her superb playing and would sometimes stop by the door to listen. And her not realizing that something more than the making of beautiful music was taking place beyond the doors!

Georgiana continued to explain that things were made awkward when they were set to travel from London to the north those months earlier. The major would be going to Lincolnshire with the colonel. Whatever they had would have to survive the test of time and distance. It reminded Catherine, though she said not a word of this, of the sad days when her eldest sister Jane was left to pine for her own true love when she remained ignored while she stayed not too far distant at her aunt and uncle's house.

That had been resolved in a most satisfactory manner. Catherine was wondering whether the same happy conclusion might be in the offing for Georgiana.

When the two officers finally came to Pemberley, it was, Georgiana said, a most happy reunion, though they attempted to be discreet, particularly in light of her brother's and Elizabeth's being overly protective of her—and her thirty thousand—and unlikely to be happy about a liaison between her and the lowly son of a city lawyer who had risen only to the rank of major, however well he performed in that role and however he was himself important for the colonel's recovery.

But an appropriate level of intimacy reappeared in their walks around Pemberley on its many paths. Over time, she had come to understand as she prepared for bed and looked out over the Pemberley Woods that she had given herself completely to Groeper and hoping against hope that he had done the same with her.

Then everything changed as if they were struck by a thunderbolt. Michael, she knew, would never in a thousand thousand years abandon the colonel, as he had proved again and again. And what did that mean for her? What did that mean for *them?* If there even was a *them.*

Yet Catherine's appearance and insistence that she would find and follow her colonel was a lifeline. Without a doubt, Georgiana, too, would go to her officer. And how could she not go as well with the woman who had become her closest, most loved friend who happened to be going precisely where she wished to go?

*　*　*　*

The weather held for the final stretch of the trip but the women's anxiousness grew with each mile to town. Now they occupied themselves with speculations of what would become of them when they found their officers— they had no doubt by this time that they would find them—and whether they would be welcomed.

They had long since rejected the suggestion that they would be deterred from their quest. *For better or worse.*

Elizabeth had made sure that the coachman knew where to deposit his charges, and the carriage rolled to a stop on Gracechurch Street.

As they were helped from the carriage, Williams, the older of the footmen, told them that "I am instructed to make meself available to you should you require anything, anything at all. A note from Mr. Gardiner will not be suspicious at the house so that is how you should write to me."

He said these were Mr. Darcy's clear instructions and he was selected for the task largely because he could read and write and that this might prove necessary.

"I will be with you in a moment, Miss Darcy, Miss Bennet, should I be required. I know why you have come, though I will not tell a soul. I pray that you will succeed. I do like and admire the two officers whatever anyone might be sayin' of 'em."

He asked the driver to wait and rang the Gardiners' bell. It was answered quickly. The butler looked very put upon at the appearance of the trio, in drab and damp and soiled clothing and the two women carrying similarly damp and soiled satchels.

"May I help you?" he said with some degree of airs.

She spoke. "I am Catherine Bennet, and this is my sister Georgiana Darcy." The butler's attitude shifted markedly. "We are being assisted by one of the Darcy footmen. I am to see my aunt and uncle. I believe they are expecting me."

The butler stepped into the house to clear the way for the visitors.

Williams and his fellow footman carried the trunks in. As they waited, he said, "Miss Bennet and Miss Darcy. Here I must leave you. You will think of what I'm tellin' you and will if necessary follow 'em, aye?"

They turned to him as he bowed, each saying nearly as one that *yes, they were infinitely appreciative for his assistance on the trip* and that *no, they would not forget his offer and kindness* and with that he and the other stepped back to the pavement and into the carriage and headed west to Brook Street.

The Gardiners' much chastened butler called for a house footman and chambermaid to join him in the foyer and barked instructions for the former to help with their satchels and the latter to fetch Mrs. Gardiner. "Mr. Gardiner is out, ladies," he said in a much improved tone.

He led them into the sitting room off the foyer and offered to get some refreshments for them, which they gladly agreed to accept. They were quite hungry, very tired, and aching to bathe and change into some proper or at least dry clothes.

Before anything could be brought to them, Mrs. Gardiner herself raced into the room. She rushed to Catherine and hugged her tightly. She immediately and happily recognized her niece's companion, from that fateful first visit to Pemberley, similarly tarnished by the travel, and squeezed her tightly as soon as she could.

The Gardiners were not in the same circles of balls and dinners and such that the Darcys were in town. Indeed, it would be hard to say that the Gardiners were in any society circle, content as they were in their comfortable home on Gracechurch Street and tending to their four children.

"We only received Elizabeth's letter an hour ago. I have sent for your uncle." She stepped back to inspect the women. "You girls are far too disordered and look very uncomfortable." She pulled a cord, and the butler entered. He was directed to have tubs made ready for the two.

"I will have your trunks sent up to your room. I am afraid you will have to share it." She looked at Georgiana, "I am afraid, Miss Darcy, that we do not have as many rooms as you may be accustomed to."

With that, she led them up to the room that had been prepared for the two of them, and they were all relieved that it was big enough and the bed was easily wide enough for them to share it, it being the only one available and the room that one or another of the Bennet girls had occupied on their many visits to town, including, in one infamous instance, for an extended period by the eldest Bennet.

38.

Neither of the officers had any notion of what was happening in Cheapside or what had happened along the road from Pemberley to London.

After his meeting with Lord Ashworth, Colonel Fitzwilliam had gone to his Regimental Club off Pall Mall. The major would be staying at his parents' house.

The club was not nearly as crowded as it had been for many years, what with the war finally and definitively over. Or at least the one on the continent. There would always be another war. Just not as yet.

The cavalry officers who frequented the place had all gone to greener or at least different pastures, each carving out such civilian jobs as they could for those beyond the relatively few allowed to remain on full active duty.

From the first evening at the club, the colonel and the major sat in the bar with their clarets after having their dinner in the officers' mess. They knew some of the others who were staying there and would often sit together late reminiscing about what had been, though the major often left shortly after dinner to return to his parents' house.

The two did not broach the real reason they were there. Instead, they spoke of looking for a new adventure, a way to keep body and soul together and maintain the control they had long had as officers in His Majesty's army.

Two or three days after their arrival in town, in the morning and before they knew of the ladies' arrival, the colonel again wondered to his friend and aide whether they might venture to America.

"We both know many who went there to fight and remained there when the war ended. To build new lives for themselves. Find an American bride. Raise an American family."

The colonel was being swept up with his ideas, the great frontier or New York there for the taking. Even for a half-blind cripple like himself.

The major's plans, though, had never accounted for that. His world would be articling in the law, being blessed by being married to Georgiana Darcy, and raising his own family in a fine neighborhood of London not far from his parents' house.

He had never thought of any speculation as the colonel was presenting to him. As they spoke, the colonel rose as quickly as he could, leaving the dining room and going to the club secretary's office. That old soldier was surprised at his visitor but was able to tell him that there was something of a roster among its members who had settled in America. He told the colonel that he could compile a list to be done with as the colonel thought fit. He promised he would have it the next day, and with a great amount of thanks, Colonel Fitzwilliam returned to the major, whose meal was gone and was sitting in a chair alone with his coffee and a copy of *The Times*.

"Well?" he asked.

"They are getting a list for me, and we will discuss it." He paused. "I did not mean to be so precipitous. My thoughts were for me alone and much as I would regret leaving you here, I cannot be the cause of the frustration of your own plans. I assure you I will be more than capable on my own."

"I appreciate that, sir. I will think on it. It comes, well, it came as a great surprise to me when you mentioned it on our trip here, but I do think it may be the most appropriate course for you to take. I cannot say that even had this recent business not come to the fore there were not as many options as we would like."

On the next day, the colonel was sitting with the major in the club's lounge before dinner, pondering yet again what was to become of him. He again insisted that Groeper not be a fool and instead look to his own situation. To read articles as his father had suggested to take up life as a lawyer. It was what the major had contemplated until things collapsed with the deaths of the Maineses.

A porter approached with a card on a highly polished silver tray.

"This is for you, Colonel Fitzwilliam," he said.

The colonel lifted it:

MARCUS GARDINER

GRACECHURCH STREET

"Gardiner," he said to the major. "I do not know any Gardiner." He passed the card to his fellow. "Do you?"

Groeper looked at it and confessed that he had no idea who it could possibly be, insisting that he knew no one by that name.

The colonel nodded to his friend and was about to return the card to the platter with instructions that this man be sent away when he remembered who he was. He was Elizabeth's, and thus Catherine's, uncle. They sat with each other before Elizabeth's wedding and, he recalled, the two had a very fine conversation. He was a man in trade but intelligent and engaging.

"Show him in," the colonel said, as he retrieved the uncle's card from the tray.

A moment later, they were shaking hands and the colonel was introducing his aide. He offered to get Gardiner a drink, and a whisky was gladly accepted as the three sat in a slight circle of three armchairs in a burgundy leather near one of the windows that looked out onto Pall Mall.

"You will understand, sir," Gardiner said after he had taken a long, pleasant drink of his whisky, "that I come on behalf of my niece Catherine Bennet."

He quickly gave the officers the news that both his niece and Darcy's sister had come to him several days earlier.

"Georgiana? Georgiana Darcy?" said the major quite astonished at this bit of information.

"The same," said Gardiner. He explained how the two ladies had appeared at his door even before he knew they were coming. "They did not and have not told me of why they have come so far in such a hurry, but Catherine said it was all to do with you."

"How did you come to find us, sir?" asked the major.

"I wish I were so clever as to have calculated that you would be here at your club. Miss Darcy said that *she* suspected you would at least visit her cousin, your brother, Colonel, and so that is where I went. Miss Darcy wrote a note to him to establish my *bona fides* and he accepted it."

The mention of a note from Miss Darcy visibly brightened the major as he listened to how this plot unfolded.

"I fear I may have, out of necessity, disclosed some...feelings of admiration that my niece on the one hand and your cousin, Colonel, on the other may have had and I convinced him that identifying where you are would not cause you any harm or difficulty. So here I am."

"Yes, sir, here you are," said the colonel, somewhat tepidly.

"And my sole charge, gentlemen, is to advise you that Miss Bennet and Miss Darcy are in town, that they are residing for the time being at my house in Cheapside, and that it is their fondest wish that you come visit them. If it must be done discreetly, it shall be done discreetly. What happens then, none of us can say."

Gardiner stood, and the others followed. He extended his hand to the colonel, who shook it and he repeated the ritual with the major.

"I hoped for but did not expect an answer right away, but I ask that you discuss it between yourselves and advise me as soon as you can so that I might advise the young ladies."

"We will," said the colonel, echoed by the major. With a bow, Gardiner turned to leave, his duty done.

As he walked towards the door, navigating through the chairs and sofas and tables set hither and thither in the large hall, his recent companions consulted and with barely the passage of a minute the major rushed to catch up.

In the club's foyer, Mr. Gardiner felt the major's hand tap his shoulder and stopped.

"Might I have a word, sir?" the major said, and extended his arm to the right, where there was a quiet corner away from the traffic that entered and departed the facility.

"Thank you for coming, sir. The colonel and I required little time to discuss the matter, and we agree that if the young ladies of whom you speak are desirous of a visit from us, it would be wrong of us to deny them their wish."

The following afternoon, as arranged, the two officers found a cab in front of the club and rode the several miles to Gracechurch Street. As it rolled to a stop in front of the Gardiners' house, its passengers saw the light curtain in the sitting room flutter with two silhouettes on either side as the curtain closed and the silhouettes vanished.

As the major paid the fare, the colonel began his distinctive walk up the stone steps that led to the ebony door with its brass knocker. But before he reached that, the door was flung open and Mr. Gardiner himself was welcoming one and then the other officer.

"They are quite nervous, I will tell you," confirmed the host. "I will leave both of you to go in."

He gave a short bow to the two and left them to it, hurrying up the stairs to inform his dear wife of what was happening, and what the pair of them thought *might* be happening in their fine sitting room.

The formality of the reunion could not and in fact did not last long. Perhaps before Mr. Gardiner had reached the first-floor landing as he went to Mrs. Gardiner, the two younger couples were bound together as they had never been before. When they eventually disentangled themselves, the ladies sat on the sofa and the men sat in the appropriate armchairs facing them.

Requests for forgiveness shot about the room like a meteor shower until they finally exhausted that emotion and turned, at the major's suggestion, to the nub of the matter. *What are we to do now?*

In fact, among them, only Georgiana and the major had bright prospects at home. Catherine and the colonel had little financially and virtually no prospects, even apart from the stigma that must forever be attached to the latter. Nor was there any easy solution to that overwhelming stigma that would attach to anyone bound to the colonel.

But that issue must be deferred until they could navigate the immediate matter of their reunions.

It was late in the afternoon. "My uncle insists that you remain for dinner," Catherine said and would hear none of the gentlemen's protests. It was an awkward meal among the six of them, the Gardiner children having been fed and left to their nighttime activities beforehand. Mr. and Mrs. Gardiner, though, proved immensely welcoming and intelligent, as Darcy had at one point mentioned to his cousin in vouching for the virtues of at least some portion of the Bennet family to which he was connecting.

The colonel, the major, and Mr. Gardiner enjoyed a fine port in the house's library as the officers were enticed to speak at least in general terms about their lives as soldiers in His Majesty's service.

It proved to be a delightful evening of the sort neither officer could have imagined just over a day before, when they were shown Mr. Gardiner's card at the club.

* * * *

Unlike Brook Street, the more commercial neighborhood of Cheapside did not allow for ready access to a park, but the Gardiners were less than a mile from St. Paul's and its fine walks and so on most days, even in foul weather, that is where they went, speaking of nothings and of everythings as they did, freed of the anxiousness that was at times overwhelming.

The colonel slept at the Regimental Club and the major at his parents', and they met each morning in the former's dining room for a breakfast and to plot out the day's events.

Time not to be wasted, when the two officers arrived on Gracechurch Street not four hours later after their midday meal one day, they asked to sit together before they went for their stroll. Catherine and Georgiana looked at one another as they went to the sitting room ahead of the others.

The major closed the door behind them. The ladies were quite nervous.

When they had found themselves as comfortable as the situation allowed in the room's familiar chairs, the colonel began.

"As you know"—he leaned forward in his chair—"decisions must be taken and soon about my future."

"*Your* future?" Catherine was quick to interject, with some vehemence.

He looked at her. "I cannot presume as to you, dearest. *I* am the one in difficulty. *I* am the one who destroyed those people's lives. I will not force you to give up your life here."

"What do you mean give up my life *here*?"

The two were now conversing oblivious to the other two in the room.

"It is the particular item that Major Groeper and I were discussing this morning and the one we must discuss with you now."

The two women's eyes went from the colonel to the major and back.

"America," said the colonel. He motioned with his hands.

Now the ladies looked at one another before repeating in unison, "America?"

"It is just our initial thought."

"You are with him on this?" It was Georgiana's turn to raise the alarm with the major.

"Georgie. I cannot say. Yes, it would alter everything I had planned, for myself and, if I'm not presumptuous, for you as well."

Georgiana rose and began to the door.

"Georgie, wait." This from Catherine. "You and I both knew this was inevitable in some ways. We must hear them out."

In something of a huff, Miss Darcy returned and plopped down on her chair. And so the discussion began.

And, as Catherine noted, the particulars may have varied, but the need for drastic steps by the colonel had to be hashed out and the extent to which they affected the other three resolved.

After they all had restless nights on it, they met again on the Saturday in the late morning. Again they sat in the sitting room on Gracechurch Street with its privacy. Catherine said she had given it much thought and they must speak to her uncle.

"I fully intend to write to my cousin about this," the colonel said, "and I may venture to sit down with my brother tomorrow after services, but I do not think expanding those aware of my predicament—"

"*Our* predicament," Catherine was quick to correct.

"Yes, *our* predicament. I do not believe that it should be expanded beyond those who absolutely need to be brought in for discussions."

"You do not know my uncle, Richard. You see him as the kind older gentleman who has brought us, Georgiana and me, to you and the major. He had very little yet built his fine business so he could afford this fine home and the servants and permit us to enjoy his fine food."

"I meant no disrespect, my dear," the colonel said after this tongue lashing. She was not deterred.

"Your cousin, Darcy, lives off an inherited country estate." She paused and turned her glance to Georgiana. "I do not mean to offend, Georgie."

"I am not offended by the truth, Catherine."

She turned back to the colonel. "And your brother is a man of science, of exhibitions and expeditions and all the Royal Societies. My uncle is a man of commerce and a successful one at that. In this new world, what are you to do as to a country estate?" As the colonel had done earlier, Catherine was rising to her oratory.

"The wars are over. The war with the United States is over. More and more second and third sons are crossing the Atlantic. Not to the plantations that have so tarnished our souls, the miserable hellholes. To New York and Philadelphia. You must speak to my uncle about it. You must convince him to suggest something useful, perhaps even allow you to form a beachhead for his firm in the United States. That is what you must do and that is what I will go to America with you to do."

She was spent from this, the others having been rendered mute by her excitement and eloquence.

"Have you spoken to him about it?" Major Groeper finally asked.

"I have not. But I am sure that he will be receptive to the idea. He has not known you for long and in some respects he has not known *me* for long, as I now am. I believe he has come to greatly respect you, for your exploits in the war and for who you have shown yourself to be to him. He has nothing but kind things to say about you since we have arrived, including after you told him what brought you here.

"He will look favorably on your proposal. I am sure of it. I am sure he has given thought to doing something in America. It being Saturday, he will be home presently. I think when he is settled in the house, you should sit with him and broach the subject. It is far better than awaiting word from Derbyshire about whatever your cousin may come up with for you to do."

"We shall go for a stroll before he does come home," suggested the major. "We could all use some air." And though it was an overcast day with a bit of a chill, that is what they did, taking their familiar route to St. Paul's.

A trio of letters arrived at Pemberley over a week after the conversation the four had at the Gardiners'. Two were directed to Fitzwilliam Darcy and one to Mrs. Fitzwilliam Darcy.

As to the former, one had the address written in an assertive script with the curious notation "OPEN THIS FIRST." The penmanship on the second envelope was in a near feminine script and it carried a similarly peculiar comment "DO NOT OPEN THIS FIRST."

Mr. and Mrs. Darcy were out when the letters arrived and the documents sat on a silver tray in the foyer until they returned, which they did together some two hours later. They were both quite curious. Darcy immediately recognized the handwriting of his cousin the colonel and of his sister. Elizabeth knew that it was Catherine who had written to her.

"This is most peculiar," she said to her husband, a sentiment with which he expressed agreement, and the two then rushed into the sitting room to open them, asking that some refreshments be brought in to them.

The letters to Darcy in order read as follows:

His Majesty's Dragoons Club
Pall Mall
London

Fitzwilliam,

> *You must forgive the tardiness of this letter, but I have much to report and have been busy making certain arrangements and taking certain decisions. Please do not share the contents of this with anyone, most particularly your wife, immediately. I make this unusual request because Elizabeth's sister*

Catherine is writing her own letter to your dear wife. I truly hope that you follow the instructions that Georgiana and I placed on our envelopes and have not read her communication to you, although much of what I have to say does concern her.

In brief, I am going to New York, and I am going with Catherine Bennet. Also coming with me is my great friend Michael Groeper—please do not overreact—he is being accompanied by your sister.

We are all, in short, to be married before we embark on our great journey to our futures.

You will surely understand the need for me to venture across the ocean to begin what must be a new life. I will not repeat the reasons. You well know them. Perhaps in time you would have suggested this to me, but I had the good fortune of my dear Catherine suggesting it to her uncle, Mr. Gardiner.

I am to be his agent in New York. As with so many others, he desires to expand and develop his business in America and New York is the place to do it. He has communicated with his corresponding bank in New York to set in motion what is needed for me to formally establish the Gardiner Trading House.

I am quite excited about the prospects of going forward, as I know so many other Englishman have done, including many an old soldier, even ones as beaten and battered as am I.

We will seek to expand to America's west but this will take some time. Mr. Gardiner has expressed every confidence that I am the man to do this, and I have gratefully accepted his kindness and the obligations he is thrusting on me.

As I hope Catherine will express to your dear wife, I believe I could not have nearly so good a chance to succeed were I to go alone. That was my initial intention, to avoid having her become entangled in my personal difficulties,. She would not hear of it. She is not her sister, but she is to me—and you must forgive me for saying so—a far more appropriate companion for a fool such as myself. I realize that I could not have recovered nearly so well as I did for all the efforts of all the doctors that tended to me without her immeasurable and regular kindness.

I can only pray that she does not realize her own grave error in falling in love with me before we are aboard the vessel that will carry us to the new world.

I will send further details to you, including about making arrangements to (perhaps discreetly) attend our wedding (which will be simultaneous to that of your dear sister).

For now, though, I ask that you wish me and your soon-to-be   sister-in-law   the   heartiest congratulations and love.

Richard

Upon finishing the surprising news he had just read, Darcy placed it down and took up the second letter sent to him, recognizing his sister's neat hand.

Gracechurch Street
London

My dearest brother,

I trust you have complied with the direction I have placed on this envelope and read the letter from our cousin before reading this. I am also sure that you will not chastise my beloved Michael Groeper for failing to obtain your blessing to our betrothal and that you will understand why it has to be so.

As Richard told you, I am to wed Michael as Richard is to wed Catherine Bennet. I know you respect Michael, and I hope that you trust me in my decision about the man I have given my heart to. I am sure you knew this before I left with Catherine. I cannot say my feelings for him are the same as yours for your dear Elizabeth, but I assure you that they are very strong indeed.

I know you will come see us in town before we are wed and you can confirm my high opinion of Major Michael Groeper, my great cavalryman and our country's hero.

Yours,
Georgiana

Mr. and Mrs. Darcy were deep into their letters but were able to look up at times to watch the other being deep into their own letter. This is what Elizabeth read.

Gracechurch Street
London

My dearest sister,

I will overwhelm you with my news. I am going to America with Colonel Fitzwilliam.

Now let me endeavour to explain myself.

You have long known of my affection for your husband's cousin. I could not help but admire his bravery when he returned from the continent and more could not help myself from believing I was blessed in aiding in his recovery. To become his nurse and then to become something more to him, as he became something more than a patient to me.

We are all unique, I know, so I do not venture to compare my love for him to your love of your dear Mr. Darcy. Or—and you will not be surprised by this as I know it is being communicated to your husband as you read this—Georgiana's for Major Groeper.

I assure you that whatever feelings she and I had when we fled Pemberley on our quest have been enhanced a thousand-fold in the presence of our two fine gentlemen. I can say no more.

I must turn to the other significant news. We are all, the four of us, going to America. I suggested to our uncle that the colonel and the major might prove of value to him in expanding his business to New York and farther afield. Uncle Gardiner had been considering such a step for some time, since the end of hostilities with both France and the United States. He is not alone in this, and it was serendipity I think that his decision to cross the waters was perfectly in alignment with the colonel's decision to seek a new opportunity in light of circumstances here in England.

Richard's letter to Darcy will have more details I think. At this point, I can only say that if there is any way for you and him to come to London to attend our wedding and perhaps see us off to America we will be forever grateful. As will Georgiana and Major Groeper.

I am,
your dear sister,
Catherine.

PS. Please keep this information close. We are certain of our course but do not know how we are to disclose it to others. It will not wait long, of course, but we hope to tell the family, including

mother and father and Mary and Jane and Bingley,
soon but must first decide on the best way to do so.

Discretion being the better part of velour, as the poet said, the dual weddings were held in a most discreet way. Those who would be the Fitzwilliams and those who would be the Groepers received a dispensation for the ceremony to be held at a small church in Cheapside, where both brides were residing for purposes of the wedding. All of the parents attended, excepting of course Georgiana's, since they were gone, but the presence of the Earl and Countess of Waddington, the earl being Georgiana's mother's brother and thus her uncle, in part made up for that.

In addition to the Darcys, Jane and Charles Bingley appeared as did the still unmarried Mary. Jane was very far along, but not too far to miss the journey and she would be at her house on Mount Street for the balance of her confinement. Lydia was in the north with her husband, who had found a position as something of a salesman for a trading firm based in Liverpool and could not make the trip. The Gardiners were there, with their four children (who occupied much of Jane's attention during the ceremony), and a post-wedding dinner was held on Gracechurch Street. As far as anyone knew, no notice of these events made it into the papers, which, while they had moved on from the scandal of the officer and the farmgirl and their bastard child, would have rekindled their interest in them were there anything worth reporting or, more exactly, which the papers themselves deemed worth reporting.

Generous provision had been made for the boy and its existence was made known with the greatest deference only to his other grandfather, who had taken the boy in and scowled at anyone who dared visit such sin as his mother might have been guilty of on the boy.

The next morning, the two couples accompanied by the Darcys went to the London docks where the four who were leaving, likely forever, boarded a tender that conveyed them to the ship that would take them to New York.

Finis

<u>Acknowledgements</u>

I appreciate the assistance provided with this book by Melissa Barbato and Juana Laucirica, both of whom read and made very helpful comments. The final product, though, is my responsibility.

<u>Waterloo</u>

I have tried to be accurate concerning the Battle of Waterloo, particularly the role of the British cavalry. General Ponsonby was killed as is described, notwithstanding the efforts of members of the Second Dragoons (Royal Scots Greys) to save him. That battle was the culmination of a number that immediately preceded it.

One of the most famous paintings about the Battle is 1881's Scotland Forever by Elizabeth Thompson, Lady Butler. (It is not in the public domain so I cannot post it here.)

The Scots Greys were among the Union Brigade, as was Colonel Fitzwilliams First Royal Dragoons. From Ireland came the Sixth Dragoons (Inniskillings). That painting, however, is considered not to be an accurate portrayal. As noted in this novel, the ground at Waterloo was very wet, which caused Bonaparte to delay his own movements, which in the end cost him.

Major Groeper's initial description of the Battle on page 83 is taken from Lt. Archibald Hamilton, 2nd (Royal North British) Regiment of Dragoons, as quoted by the National Army Museum in a piece on Famous Calvary Charges.

A Vindication of the Rights of Woman

In her section 5.2 of her seminal 1792 work *A Vindication of the Rights of Woman*, Mary Wollstonecraft refers to *Fordyce's Sermons*, which are mentioned by Mr. Collins in *Pride and Prejudice*. She is not a fan. Her discussion begins:

> *Dr. Fordyce's sermons have long made a part of a young woman's library; nay, girls at school are allowed to read them; but I should instantly dismiss them from my pupil's, if I wished to strengthen her understanding, by leading her to form sound principles on a broad basis; or, were I only anxious to cultivate her taste; though they must be allowed to contain many sensible observations.*

You can download a free copy here.

More to the point of this story is her description in Chapter 2 of the education of soldiers, which she compares to the education received by women, a description that in part colors my own of Colonel Fitzwilliam:

> *As a proof that education gives this appearance of weakness to females, we may instance the example of military men, who are, like them, sent into the world before their minds have been stored with knowledge or fortified by principles. The consequences are similar; soldiers acquire a little superficial knowledge, snatched from the muddy current of conversation, and, from continually mixing with society, they gain, what is termed a knowledge of the world; and this acquaintance with manners and customs has frequently been confounded with a knowledge of the human heart.*

But can the crude fruit of casual observation, never brought to the test of judgment, formed by comparing speculation and experience, deserve such a distinction? Soldiers, as well as women, practice the minor virtues with punctilious politeness. Where is then the sexual difference, when the education has been the same; all the difference that I can discern, arises from the superior advantage of liberty which enables the former to see more of life.

To be clear, I am no scholar of this or of Wollstonecraft—who died of complications related to giving birth to the girl who would become Mary Shelley—but find these minor aspects interesting.

_The Omen at Rosings Park: How
Elizabeth Became Mrs. Darcy_

The Diary of Elizabeth Elliot

Austen Erotica: Anne and Charlotte

Contemporary

I Am Alex Locus: My Search for the Truth
(set chiefly on the Upper West Side and in Bronxville,
NY)

<u>Gilded Age</u>

<u>*Róisín Campbell: An Irishwoman in New York*</u>

<u>*A Studio on Bleecker Street*</u>

A Maid's Life

As J.P. Garland (Romances)

Coming to Terms

Disowned

A Theory About Valentine's Day

A Vintage Gown* (*and the women who own it)

An American Historian on Oxford's High Street

A Fairytale of New York

Accidently in Love

The Prodigal Daughter

An International Exchange

DermodyHouse.com